PREACHER AND CO

A STAINED...GLASS FAMILY

BY

BRENDON BOONE

Millar Press
International

A Kaleidoscope

OF AUTHORS

FROM MANY VOICES COMES ONE SAGA...
AN HALF-CENTURY IN THE MAKING.

Millar Press International
155 Dowlin Forge Road, Suite B
Downingtown, PA 19335

Published 2018 by Millar Press International

Printed in the United States of America

20 19 18   1 2 3 4

ISBN 978-1-7321717-1-8 (hard back edition)
ISBN 978-1-7321717-0-1 (Limited Collector's Edition)
Library of Congress Control Number: 2018939073

FOR

BRO YO

Winner of the Golden Boot Award
ANDREW J. FENADY
Author of *Double Eagles*
RIDERS TO MOON ROCK

MULTITALENTED BRENDON BOONE, reputed actor, now has sailed into the seas of authorship with PREACHER AND CO, a western packed with passion, conflict, action and humanity.

His literary creations of 'Campbell McCool' and 'Tademus Co' are worthy of a continuing western series. I've written a few westerns, myself, and look forward to reading their further adventures.

Brendon, welcome to the scribblers' club and write on!

—Andrew J. Fenady

[Legend has it that Brendon was the model for this cowboy on horseback in Red Rock Canyon, used subsequently as one of the locations in THE HANGED MAN, starring Brendon, along with Steve Forrest, Cameron Mitchell (both, as Brendon, sons of preachers), Will Geer and Dean Jagger.]

A solidly engrossing and compelling literary and motion picture concept possessing highly marketable ingredients, particularly in view of current trends. It is an outstandingly entertaining property, laced with richly redeeming social significance and embracing thoroughly personable leads in the characters of 'Campbell' and 'Tademus'. There is evoked a warmth, a sense of humanity - a brotherhood, if you will. There is comedy, humor and lightheartedness. There is tragedy and pathos - drama, conflict, suspense and action. All these elements embodied in this post-Civil War setting furnish a most propitious backdrop for the dramatization of themes bearing remarkable pertinence to the climate reflective of may issues and concerns of today.

There is an enormous audience primed and anxious to receive and to become acquainted with PREACHER AND CO. We have an opportunity, if not indeed an obligation, to reach that audience with this acquaintance - one which holds every potential for proving to be an entertaining and inspirational enrichment.

Signed:

Robert E. Lee

Ulysses S. Grant

Mississippi's 'grand dame' of literature and
Pulitzer Prize-winner Eudora Welty encouraged:
"You MUST write this book, Brendon!"

For my parents, Norman and Leola, for life

My friend, Campbell,
From the past to the present

My son, Norman Brendon III,
From the present to the future

My lady, Kueen Bee Karen,
From the future and beyond-

And for all eternity!

How many vivid tales told in many a century have ended in a wedding! And they have so ended precisely because they promised happy beginnings. But there can come tragedy so complete that it brings to an utter end the stately and beautiful rhythm of family life.

Revelation 18:23

Interpreter's Bible
exposition by
Lynn Harold Hough

Papa had a
mule and he let
me ride it.

Then Papa told me
the story of
Preacher and Co.

Author's Note

IN THE NARRATIVE TO FOLLOW, my PREACHER AND CO story begins with tales told fireside by Grandpa Boone after I'd unlaced his Brogans for him and bathed his tired feet drawn from his having trod the south forty all day plowing-up God's good earth. With a slight smile of amusement at me he'd gaze through his cocked eye (won in a knife fight defending the honor of his new "Yankee" bride, Mamie Baker Boone, whom he'd brought down to Mississippi from her Indiana home). This is where a connection with my fellow thespian, James Byron Dean, began but I get ahead of my saga. Those connections were later to be established via my film-acting career and did prove to be substantive, but that'll come later in an autobiography —

IT WAS A GOOD REHEARSAL... NOW LET'S SHOOT IT!

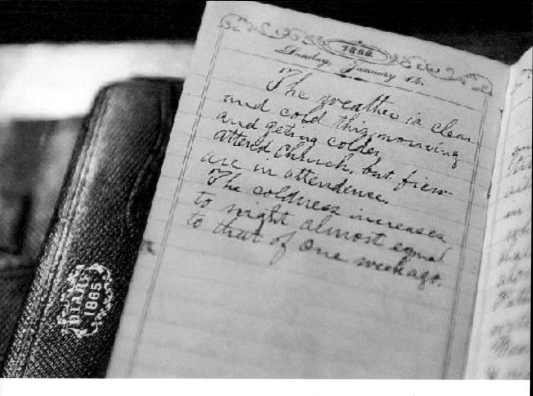

Based upon realities lived and journals dug from
Mississippi's Civil War battlefields...

this story happened!!!

Once upon a tyme...

CHAPTERS

AN END LEADS TO
A BEGINNING

CHAPTER

THE FOG PUSHED IN off Mobile Bay and smothered everything in a thick, wet blanket, just as it had done every night for a week. It reeked of rotting fish and gun powder. It dripped from his straggly hair and trickled down his face in rivulets that settled in the corners of his mouth and tasted like tears. It made his uniform, what was left of it, a wet, chafing torment. Swiping a soggy sleeve across his face left yet another streak of mud. With only his cupped hands as a tool, Cam McCool once again bailed out the brine that incessantly seeped through the sand and into the shallow trench that was his refuge. He dared not rub at his burning eyes. The first time he'd done that was lesson enough. It took a long time, and too much precious fresh water, finally to rinse out the sand.

With most of the standing water temporarily removed, Davis Campbell McCool, educated farmer and physician, slumped back into the cold, damp niche he had carved out for himself, and wondered at the machinations of fate that had led him to this God-forsaken stretch of gritty hell at the edge of Mobile Bay. A mere six years earlier, in the Year of Our Lord 1859, he had proudly graduated from Atlanta Medical College. Now it seemed like a lifetime ago. As a newly-minted doctor, full of all the hope and ambition of a young man still inexperienced in the world, he'd eagerly headed back home to Mossy Point, Mississippi, wanting nothing more than to heal the sick and ease the suffering of the people in the community he loved.

Then the Federates had attacked Fort Sumpter. That was April, 1861.

Campbell had conscientiously, if not eagerly, accepted his responsibility and enlisted in the Confederate Army leaving behind his bride and their infant son. But it was for the sole purpose of saving lives, not taking them. He had given it his all, desperately attempting to save the limbs and lives of horribly shattered boys with only the barest minimum of vital tools, supplies and assistance. Even in his most vivid nightmares, he couldn't conjure the kind of hell that was spitting out this level of carnage. Still, he rose to the rank of Chief Surgeon at the Confederate Army Hospital just outside Savannah, Georgia.

In August, 1863, Campbell had been transferred to the front in Mississippi, where he joined General William E. (Billy) Lampton at Mississippi Springs. Since that time, almost two years now, he'd served the battered and retreating Confederate troops that were pitted against the combined onslaught of Generals Hurlbut and Halleck, as the Union armies took siege of Natchez, then Vicksburg, and finally the state capital of Jackson. More and more, during this past year, he had been pulled away from the agony and death in the field hospital and given a weapon, soldiers being the more desperately needed commodity. And steadily his saving of lives had been replaced with his taking of them. It was then that he'd experienced first hand just what kind of agony man could inflict on his fellow man.

The Confederate defenders had been driven back by the growing swath of the unstoppable Union tide under General William T. Sherman, now bringing them to be dug into these sad excuses for trenches along the Mobile Bay with their backs to the Gulf of Mexico or the 'Grand Gulf' as his fellow Mississippians thought of it. All night long on this the ninth day of the entrenchment, the impersonal cannon exchange had lit up the starless skies in some sort of eerie blaze of glory though the spectacular display could hardly be witnessed as anything glorious. Man, in this gory perpetuation of war, had masked the majesty of the Almighty and camouflaged the twinkling of His heavens with his own illumination of terrible destruction.

As to exactly why the opposing commanders had chosen only the nighttime to engage in their fighting, Cam could only speculate. Perhaps the harshness of daylight made the futility of it all too apparent. Perhaps, in the harsh light of day, the faces of the foe became too visible and the battle, then, too personal. Whatever the reasons might have been, the daylight hours of the last week had been reserved for sleeping, such as one could claim it, while only token sentries remained posted along both lines.

The black of night was reserved for the exchanges of war. It was far less personal to hurl a cannonball out into the darkness than it was to spear an opponent with one's bayonet, face to face. No matter how all the justifications of war were eventually sorted out and organized, however, Cam knew that no participant in this Civil War could escape still whole in mind, body or spirit.

As he watched the sun inch its way above the horizon, he wrapped his arms more tightly around himself, hugging his rifle to his chest as if it could provide some semblance of warmth, and listened to the sounds around him in the wet gloom—the loading of a rifle, soft murmurings of men's voices, possibly in prayer—a deep, consumptive cough that his clinical mind told him would bring a painful end to Corporal Jenkins' young life. And he couldn't do a damned thing about it.

The brightening morning promised to burn-off the fog, and he anticipated the coming heat of the day with the hope that it would help to ward off the chill that had settled into his bones and his soul. How far man had fallen from the graces of God, Cam meditated. Was there still a path back to His grace, a way past the years of hate and hurt and despair? What would his father be preaching from the pulpit this Sabbath, were he still alive?

At the thought of his parents, gone now these past six months, an unexpected knot tightened his throat. His father had carried on even, as week after week, news of tragedy and ruin from the front lines continued to pour in. From the modest pulpit of the Mossy Point Christian Church, the good Reverend Emmett McCool had shared the promise of God's unrelenting love and forgiveness of his flawed children. How could Campbell do any less?

As the sun rose high enough to warm his face, he felt a calm envelope him like the fog off the bay—quiet and still. It was a peacefulness of mind and spirit totally inconsistent with his present surroundings yet still as warm as the rising Spring sunshine. Campbell breathed deeply of the salty, acrid air and bowed his head. He understood clearly now what his path would be to healing and redemption. This God-forsaken madness had taken his father's life, but it couldn't take his voice or his message.

The shouting startled Cam out of his reverie. A rider in a tattered butternut uniform raced out of the mist along the line of trenches, his rangy steed throwing off flecks of sweat. "It's all over, boys! Lee surrendered to Grant. Happened at Appomattox, Virginny 'round about noon yesterday.

Confirmation's in, it's official, it's all done. General Lee surrendered."

Then the rider and his shouts trailed from earshot down the beach.

It was all over. The single thing he had prayed for every day for four interminable years had come to pass. He had imagined it would be a more momentous event, maybe accompanied by marching bands and dancing in the streets. To be still huddled in this miserable trench seemed surreal. But he knew that it was all really just the beginning—the reconstruction, the reuniting, the rehealing. If this brutal conflict were to serve any redeeming purpose, the real fight had not yet begun.

There had been wars before. There would be wars again. Yet this one seemed to have carried an uniqueness all its own. It was a war of ideologies. Brother had stepped across the geographical and philosophical lines to oppose brother, with families torn apart in the conflict, the prime issues being man's ongoing inhumanity to man. Be all that as it may, it was for everyone now to come together in a brotherhood of man, under the fellowship of God. Man's natural instinct certainly couldn't be enslavement of his fellow man but rather love for him as a brother. He knew what his father would have been preaching this first war-free Sabbath in four years. Campbell surged again with his renewed sense of purpose.

Although his soul awakened with new determination, his body and mind were numbed and weaken by days of battle, months of deprivation, years of frustration and tribulation. He had to use his rifle as a crutch to pry himself from the mud and sand. Laboriously, he lifted himself to an erect stance and climbed from the trench to bathe in the warmth of the morning sun. Then he turned and walked slowly across the sandbar toward the thicket of the woods, away from the bloody, cratered beach.

He had not stopped to think about where he was headed. He just needed to be away from the fighting and fear. He needed to curl into a ball somewhere warm and dry and sleep for a month, feeling nothing, thinking of nothing. All around him were Confederate and Federate troops alike, just as dazed as he, now ignoring opposing colors as they set about the grim ritual of caring for their wounded and burying their dead. Mocking, still-smoking cannons sat unmanned. Campbell stepped over the bodies, gazed at the ashen faces, the horrible results of the final fight. All of it washed over him like the waves of a nightmare. He reached the edge of the woods and continued his mindless slog, working his way through the thick underbrush.

After stumbling and falling through the forest for some two hundred yards amid only the sounds of tree limbs and bushes slapping against his intrusion, and the occasional crackling of underbrush beneath his steps, his feeling of acute aloneness was suddenly shattered.

"Just hold it right there, Reb," a voice behind him warned. "No need you turnin' around neither."

Campbell halted in his tracks, holding his rifle loosely at his side. Two young Union soldiers emerged from the foliage about ten feet behind him. The 'talker' of the two resumed. "You can just let that rifle drop, too, whilst you're at it."

With a slow exhale of futility, Campbell released the rifle, and it hit the ground with a soft thud.

The spokesman addressed his companion. "Marly, m' boy, I think we done snatched us a yellow-bellied deserter. Reckons how now we might's well just go ahead on and shoot him right here. Just spare them the bother later on. What you got to say to that, Johnny Reb?"

Still with his back to his challengers, Campbell sighed deeply. "The war's finished, friend."

"Well, well, well, now ain't that there just something though. And what you know about that. This here Reb's already calling us his 'friends' even."

The boy's companion finally intervened. "Leave him be, Lucas."

But Lucas would not be dissuaded. "Not 'til I git my last 'graycoat', it ain't over."

Campbell tensed at the sound of a firing pin clicking back. There was sudden commotion and a shout. "No, Lucas! You can't do th…"

The rifle discharged wildly. Responding instinctively Campbell wheeled around, drew his handgun and fired. The bullet found its mark, ripping into the upper back of the lad who was trying to stop the action.

Time and motion froze. Lucas hunched, clasping his injured friend to his chest with his eyes widened in disbelief. Campbell stood transfixed, his arm still extended in firing position. Then the wounded soldier slithered from Lucas' arms and slumped to the ground. Lucas remained riveted to the spot, staring down the barrel of Campbell's pistol. He lifted his eyes from the gun to Campbell's face, eyes wide in terror, looking for some reading in his expression. There was none. Campbell was stunned, the horror of what had just happened struggling to sink into his consciousness.

Like a hot tide, the blood flushed back into Campbell's brain as he sobered to reality. His arm fell to his side and his fingers released the weapon.

Lucas backed off a couple of paces from his buddy's fallen form at his feet, then turned and lit off into the woods, disappearing into the undergrowth as quickly as he'd appeared

Blood pumped from the young Yank's wound at an alarming rate. Campbell rushed to his side, and kneeling, lifted the boy's head gently onto his lap. He pressed his hand over the gaping exit wound in the boy's chest, fully aware that his efforts would make no difference.

With a childlike expression of hope and anticipation, the boy weakly asked, "Is it really all over...?"

Something hard closed off Campbell's throat, and he could only nod.

The boy started trying to pull something from inside his jacket. Campbell helped him retrieve an old, faded tintype. Smeared now with blood, it was a portrait of a family gathered in their Sunday best, posing stoically for the camera, to record some happy occasion.

As Campbell watched the life drain away, the boy spoke faintly. "Well, I'd best be gettin' on back home... now... then..." He stopped speaking, but his eyes remained in their gaze into Campbell's, unfocused and unseeing. Campbell knew he was gone.

Cam eased the eyelids down over the dead eyes, carefully lay the boy's head on the ground, and pushed himself to his feet. He shuffled over a few paces until he stood over his rifle. He bent down and, with measured moves, grasped the barrel and lifted it off the ground. It felt inordinately heavy, almost too much weight to bear. The metal barrel was cold in his bloody hands.

His anger rose like a tidal wave, submerging all conscious thought, blurring his vision with stinging tears. Something feral reared from a dark hole inside him and grabbed hold. With more strength than he thought he had left, he swung the weapon in a wide arc, slamming it against the nearest tree. Again and again and again, the stock pounded the tree, splinters of both flying in all directions. When the stock was reduced to shreds, he continued the assault with the barrel, until it was just mangled iron in his fists.

The wave of anger and despondency, the molten rage at the senselessness of it all, dissipated as quickly as it had hit, leaving him breathless and weak. He twisted and slumped helplessly, with his back against the lacerated tree, and collapsed to the ground. Before him lay the body of the young Yank who would never again share a happy occasion with his family.

Hours passed. Night finally curtained the forests, and a reverent tranquillity seemed to permeate. Even the sounds of the crickets tendered a soft funereal dirge. He lost track of time. Had he slept? He didn't know, nor did he care. Gradually the night sounds yielded to the birds' chirping promise of another new day. Sunlight began to bathe the branches, casting long shadows, and shining on Campbell's face, rousing him. He blinked his eyes against the brightness, then held them open, unblinking, forcing himself finally, truly to look at the dead boy lying only feet away. With a deep breath, he rose from his position against the tree and faced the reality of yesterday, surrounded by both death and the new day's awakening life. He dug through the boy's knapsack until he found the small digging tool, then, selecting a grassy mound among the towering pines, he dug a grave.

The effort drove the stiffness from his muscles, and the fog from his mind. When the chore was done, he gathered up the boy's personal effects, including the tintype, and gently lifted the slight, frail body from the spot where its soul had left it. He must've once been a strapping lad, but the depravations of war had left him rail thin and nearly weightless. Cam carefully lowered the body into the ground, and began returning the freshly turned soil to its place. He selected two sturdy branches from a fallen pine, and using his knife and the young soldier's boot laces, he fashioned a serviceable cross. He took a moment to tidy up the ground around the grave, pushing away leaves and debris, then gently pressed the crude cross into the ground at its head.

Stepping back and bowing his head, Campbell recited: "For the Lord is my Shepherd; I shall not want. He maketh me to lie down in green pastures. He leadeth me beside still waters.

He restoreth my soul. He leadth me in the paths of righteousness for His name's sake. Yea, though I walk through the valley of the shadow of death, I will fear no evil for Thou art with me. Thy rod and Thy staff, they comfort me. Thou preparest a table before me in the presence of mine enemies. Thou anointest my head with oil; my cup runneth over. Surely goodness and mercy shall follow me all the days of my life, and I will dwell in the house of the Lord forever. Amen."

These last rites done, Campbell turned from the gravesite with an overpowering sense that the boy's spirit had already preceded him.

MOSSY POINT, MISSISSIPPI

CHAPTER

2

CAM HAD NOT WALKED FOR LONG through the growing heat of the morning before he had to stop and rest next to a creek and try to abate the rumblings of his empty stomach with water. It was next to this unnamed little stream that God chose to smile on him and his aching feet. A roan mare, still in full tack, was also enjoying the burbling waters. She looked up at him with soulful dark eyes as he slowly approached, and greeted him with a soft nicker.

Her ribs were prominent, and she needed a good currying, but she gentled at his touch and seemed to enjoy a good ear scratch and nose rub.

"Where's your soldier, girl? Did he go off and leave you?" Cam looked around for her rider, but aside from the birds, the two of them were alone in the green woodland. She was one of the victims of the war, too, Cam mused. There were probably many riderless horses left to their own devices now that hostilities had ended.

Though old and scuffed, the bridle and saddle were well made and sturdy. He rummaged through the unmarked saddlebags and came up with a stale Johnny-cake wrapped in a grimy bandana, a handful of loose oats, a well-thumbed but otherwise unmarked Bible, and a one-page letter addressed to 'Dearest' and signed 'Annie'. Feeling like a peeping Tom,

Campbell skimmed over the neatly penned text, but it was sadly brief and discussed only the death of a hunting dog.

"I reckon you and I were meant to be together," Cam told the horse, feeding her the handful of oats as he bit into the cornmeal cake. "If we're to be traveling companions, you'll need a proper name. How does Annie sound to you?"

As if in reply, the mare snorted and shook her head.

Although Mossy Point, Mississippi, the only place Cam had ever called home, was only 40-odd miles from where the end of the war had dumped him, on the beach near Mobile, the ride took him three days. He stopped often at meadows of wildflowers and new green grass to let the horse forage while he'd dip a makeshift fishing line into a stream to catch dinner. He tried to convince himself that he wasn't purposefully delaying his arrival at what he knew would be a nearly unbearable scene. Military reports had braced him, toward the end of last year, that there would be no home as he remembered it, and as he had left it, to which he could return. Mossy Point, along with Pascagoula, Bay St. Louis, Biloxi, Ocean Springs, all of them settlements along Mississippi's Grand Gulf Coast, had fallen late victims to the bombardments from Admiral Farragut's fleet.

Those last five miles leading to the old family homestead were the hardest. They led Campbell down the all too familiar Hanging Moss Road, so-named for its canopy draping from the trees which lined both sides. This had been the setting of so many of his early boyhood fantasies, and he smiled slightly at the memories. Among these ancient live oaks he'd been Robin Hood saving fair Maid Marian, and Saint George slaying the fire-breathing dragon, as well as countless other mythical identities.

Around the last familiar bend, Campbell came upon the sight he had been dreading. The twin field stone chimneys, standing tall like tireless and indestructible sentinels, were separated by some thirty yards. Collapsed between them was the blackened rubble of the once modest but comfortable homestead now reduced to ashes and charcoal. Flanking the clearing was the still-erect smokehouse. Ironic, he thought, that the smokehouse had escaped the flames.

The mare stood reverently motionless beneath him, as if she sensed his sorrow. Finally Cam shook himself free of his trance and dismounted, letting the reins drag on the sooty ground, and proceeded to pace cautiously through the debris.

Near one of the stone fireplaces, he knelt down and grubbed about in the ashes, searching for what he knew must still be there. After moving several charred beams out of the way, and using a piece of one as a crude shovel, he unearthed a small, molding trunk which he gently lifted and set in front of him. He pried open the latches and began exploring its contents.

On top was a bundle of his own letters to his folks, now neatly tied together with a faded red ribbon. Beneath them was the aged family Bible. He carefully turned back its binding to reveal, on the designated page, the family tree. In several different precise, practiced hands, inscriptions outlined the names, dates and places of birth, marriages, and deaths, of some half dozen generations of McCools, including the most recent in his mother's small, shaky script. Campbell had been maintaining control of his emotions so far, but now he couldn't prevent his eyes from brimming with tears as he remembered all the times and all the loved ones. He closed the ancient, fading cover and set the Bible aside.

Next he removed the old family album in its faded red worn-velvet binding. Gently he turned the brittle pages, which contained a collection of photographs taken of the McCools through the years. There was the antiquated Daguerreotype of his parents that they'd splurged on when the first photographic shop opened up in town. Unmounted to a page but stuck between two were larger tintypes. One was of Campbell with his bride, Mary Frances, at his medical school commencement; the other was their wedding photograph.

MAY 1, 1859

The sight of her standing before him in the long, gauzy nightgown was an image he wished he could save and savor forever. Even when she'd dressed in her most glittering party gowns, she'd never looked more radiant, her smile had never been so alluring, or the scent of her so close and intimate. At that moment, Campbell's heart swelled with such joy and pride that he thought it would explode right out of his chest. Mary Frances Ashmore, the sultry, dark-haired belle of every society ball, the envy of every Atlanta debutante, was now Mrs. Davis Campbell McCool. The truth of it had yet to sink in.

He'd met her at a Christmas party that one of his medical school classmates had coerced him into attending, and she'd immediately taken his breath away, along with his heart. Every time he worked up the nerve to invite her to a ball or the theater, he was amazed that she accepted, and during those final months of school, they had been inseparable, even turning up a time or two as an item on the society page of the <u>Daily Intelligencer</u>. When she was on his arm, all eyes were on them, and he felt as if he could take on the world. The night he'd gotten down on one knee and asked her to share his life with him had been one of the most nerve-wracking of his life. When she'd joyfully accepted, he was sure he was in Heaven.

Their marriage ceremony had taken place that morning, scarcely five months after they'd met, at the Mossy Point

Christian Church. Soft candlelight cast a warm, hazy glow over them as they knelt before the altar, surrounded by the wedding party of some two dozen family members, with Cam's father officiating. It was so filled with hope and promise.

"Campbell, dear. . ." Her soft voice pulled him from his reverie, as she encircled his neck with her arms and pressed against him. "Are you going to stand here drooling like an idiot all night?"

He breathed in her scent, and it only fueled his arousal. He kissed her deeply, felt her mold against him and answer his ardor with her own. He lifted her gently onto the bed, swiftly removed the remainder of his own clothes, and joined her beneath the sheets.

She pulled him to her and kissed his ear, then whispered, "I have a confession."

"Do tell, Mrs. McCool," he murmured, covering her neck with light nibbles.

"You are not my first."

He raised himself up on one elbow to look into her shining dark eyes and smiled back at her. "Your first what?" he teased. "But your only love," he added.

Her giggle quickly turned into a deep moan.

They didn't get a lot of sleep that night, but Campbell wasn't complaining. As he lay awake in the darkness, face to face with his sleeping wife, he studied her perfect features—her wide-set eyes with the long, dark lashes curled against her pale, high cheekbones, her straight, aristocratic nose with just a hint of an impish up-tilt, and her small mouth with those generous, soft, pink lips. She was, indeed, a beauty, and she would undoubtedly be the mother of handsome sons and lovely daughters, if his own somewhat unsymmetrical features didn't muddle the mix too badly.

Her eyes fluttered open and she smiled at him. "What are you staring at, Doctor?"

"You. I am seeing our unborn children in your eyes."

"Are they speaking to you?" she teased.

"They're saying that they have the most beautiful, intelligent, loving mother any child could wish for, and they'd like to have another cookie, please."

Her laughter was music in the dark room. "They've learned well from their father that flattery will get them everywhere." Her lips caressed his lightly, then she pulled back, her smile fading. "You will be such a wonderful father. Let's have lots and lots of little McCools running around begging for cookies."

"Dozens," he agreed, easing her beneath him again to melt into her heat.

Campbell recalled advice from his clergyman father, "Don't ever take her laughter away." He slammed the picture album closed, sending up a cloud of dust and ashes. The memory was like a knife to his chest, the pain intense and physical. He shoved it back into the darkest part of his mind with just as much force, and turned back to the contents of the trunk.

Laying underneath everything, almost invisible against the dark bottom of the trunk, was a leather-bound portfolio he didn't remember ever seeing before. Compared to the trunk's other contents, it looked almost new with a finely tooled and gold-embossed cover. His curiosity piqued, he sat back and crossed his legs, laying it across his lap. When he opened it, he smiled. They had lovingly saved his poetry.

Eons ago, back in his innocent, vainglorious youth, back before the world went mad, he'd considered himself a talented word-smith to rival the likes of Whitman and Wordsworth. Even the local newspaper had published a couple of his nicer pieces. Without his knowledge, his mother had neatly copied his work onto fine parchment and folded them into this expensive portfolio, to save for posterity. The one resting on top was a personal favorite, and he read it now, allowing himself to return, at least in his mind, to a better time.

MY FATHER

God blessed me early in life
before I could even account.
I was born into his *F*amily
with love in fullest amount.

Soon I recognized my beginning
and reflected upon my fate;
Yet, seeing through wiser eyes
caused me *A*dmiration to take.

I was then to be instructed
that life is lived by mere man -
in which unique arrangement
as much *T*olerance is needed as there's sand.

But then as mind expanded
another seed was sown -
Instead of my nurturing despair,
*H*ope in its place was grown.

With all these inspirations
which have been mine to share,
there's promise of all *E*ternity
when life is lived with care.

So now my prayer becomes
that as I move along -
this *R*everence that's instilled in me
in others may, too, belong.

Cam ran his fingers lightly over the carefully printed words. He'd written it as a fiftieth birthday present for his father, laboring over every word to get it just right—to make it say all the things he felt in his heart but had never been able to express to the man's face. When his father had read it aloud to the gathering of well-wishers at the party his congregation had thrown for him, Campbell had hidden behind the refreshment table, wishing he could fall through the floor.

With a rare, excited anticipation, he lifted the corner of the thick parchment sheet and turned it over to see which of his other poems his mother had seen fit to preserve. All he had to see was the title, printed boldly in capital letters, mocking him from the page. "Anniversary Ode". He'd written it for Mary Frances for their second anniversary, just days after he'd left her standing on the main street of Mossy Point, clutching their child to her breast, her beautiful features wet with tears and distorted in anguish. The cause seemed so noble then, and the war wasn't going to last very long...

He slapped the portfolio cover closed without reading another word. He'd known it by heart at one time. But that part of his heart had been ripped away.

Setting the portfolio in the ashes beside him, he lastly pulled a heavy leather pouch from a deep corner, and quickly checked its contents. His father had stashed away enough gold to get him started on his mission, if he were frugal, and he said a quick prayer of thanks for his father's wise planning. Placing the leather pouch inside his jacket front, he returned most of the other contents to the chest, closed the lid, and reburied it in the hole beneath the ashes. Crawling away to the opposite corner of the ruins, Cam dug a suitable place of interment for the wedding picture and buried it deep. He rose stiffly and stepped gingerly through the ruins to retrieve the portfolio. It spoke to him, begging him not to rebury it with everything else. Sometime, somewhere, he may need to read all those words again. Then he walked away from his home for the last time.

Some fifty yards away, he approached the family cemetery, cordoned off by a three-foot high wrought-iron grilled fencing. Cam stepped over the low fence and moved over toward a broad granite tombstone bearing two fresh carvings, side by side.

Catherine McCool

Beloved wife and mother

Born August 27, 1802 - Died November 4, 1864

Emmett McCool

Beloved husband and father

Born March 6, 1798 - Died November 4, 1864

The hard, visceral reality of the cold, grey stone was the final blow that broke through Cam's hard-fought attempts at control. His legs gave out beneath him, and he crumpled to the ground, coming to sit among the overgrown weeds and wildflowers. His hands covering his face, he sobbed as he had not done since that night he'd received his father's last letter. There was so much he'd missed, so much he still needed. Sage advice left untendered, the warmth of hugs never given, words he meant to say one day, not realizing that day was never to be. And the laughter of innocent children silenced forever.

When the horse whinnied at some unseen annoyance, Campbell finally raised his head and rubbed at his eyes with the heels of his hands. He took a minute to let his eyes wander the small family plot which once had been so reverently cared for and tended. His grandparents were here along with two uncles and his younger sister Myrle who had not lived to see her first birthday. But Mary Frances and the child were buried elsewhere, away from the McCool family's loving embrace.

The purpose and commitment felt as he occupied the trenches along Mobile Bay now, at the final resting place of his Pa who had originally inspired them, Cam experienced resurging from the very depths of his soul.

The day's shadows were growing long, and there was indeed much more to say, so much more to witness for anyone who might listen to him. He had a mission to complete and a ministry to pursue. Reluctantly extracting himself from this communion with family, Campbell managed to lift himself from his knees to his feet. Nestling the portfolio into his saddlebag, he swung onto Annie and guided her back through the cathedral-like canopy of Hanging Moss Road.

TADEMUS CO

CHAPTER

3

As Campbell and his sturdy little roan trekked northward, he grew more enthralled with his plans. During those cool, damp nights and the warming spring days, God had blessed him with fine weather, and he saw his future stretched before him like a glowing sunrise.

On a couple of occasions, when he'd been unable to hook a fish or snare a rabbit, he'd abased himself to 'borrow' from the diminished larder of farmsteads he passed, always leaving a token coin in appreciation, and a note. He never took much, as he had no desire to deprive anyone of what little they had left—just a couple of handfuls of grain or an egg or two, enough to sustain himself and the horse for another day. They'd both lived with hunger and want long enough that it was no stranger to them.

Along with his challenge of 'sharing the faith' toward enriching any congregants willing to listen, lingering all but to the point of obsession was the abiding mission of his seeking out the family of the young Yank whose life he'd so tragically claimed. He hoped someday to help them reconcile to their son's not having returned from the war, and to help ease somehow the pain of their loss. It was something he felt compelled to do were he ever to find peace again within his own heart. Perhaps God could forgive him, but he could not forgive himself.

Meanwhile, he hoped along with the Lord's forgiveness he might, likewise, find inspiration toward bringing His words of salvation and hope to the war-ravaged citizenry along his trek northward. As he swayed with Annie's steady gait, he composed in his mind his first message. He would use as his text, 'For Christ sayeth, it is through Me that thou shalt inherit eternal life', a passage he was feeling a special affinity for recently. But first he needed a few supplies.

On the high street in Biloxi, he came across a small newspaper office, and stopped to barter for what he needed. Without having to surrender too much of the precious gold from his father's pouch, he purchased newsprint, a pen and some ink. At the Baptist church several blocks down, he was prepared to relinquish yet more of his gold for a few hymnals, but after explaining what he wanted them for, the wizened little pastor had given him a half dozen, refusing to take any compensation for them. He'd clasped Cam's hands in his gnarled, calloused ones, and assured him that any souls he was able to save with the worn song books would be payment enough. Cam had thanked him, and prayed with him, and then moved on with a renewed encouragement for his broken country.

It was on a hot, humid Saturday morning that Cam arrived in Sandy Hook, Mississippi, a little settlement which had remained about as unharmed as any throughout this part of the South. It lay nestled just outside Columbia, on the banks of the Pearl River which ran some 60 miles east, parallel to the mighty Mississippi. Settling cross-legged under an oak beside the peaceful river, Cam let Annie graze in the meadow as he planned his first efforts as a circuit preacher. He tore the fragile newsprint into as many individual sheets as he could, leaving them at least large enough to be noticeable. Then, setting the bottle of ink in the grass next to him and using his saddlebags as a lap desk, he mustered his best penmanship and wrote out some flyers.

Preaching and Worship-Sunday Evenings
Forbes Landing, Pearl River
No Baptizing. All Welcome. All Come.

He spent the afternoon posting the notices all around Sandy Hook and Columbia, in any shop where he was permitted to do so. Surely by tomorrow evening a large congregation would have assembled at Forbes Landing and be eager to worship and to receive God's word.

There had to be more to being free than this. In all those whispered, secret conversations, the grownups always talked about how glorious it would be. It was the Promised Land, and once they got there, there'd be singing and dancing and honey flowing in the streets, and everyone would be happy and healthy and carefree. Tademus Co was just bored.

Now that Massah Ed was dead, and the Young Massah and the overseer had run off somewhere, he didn't have to work in the fields anymore, or clean the latrines, or slop the hogs (because they were all dead, too). Only Mammy June and One-Eyed Jake were still hanging around what was left of the plantation, now that the big house was burnt down and because they were just too old to start being free now. He helped them out around what was left of the slave cabins and they kept him fed, but he really had to find out for himself what this 'freedom' thing was all about.

Tad pushed himself farther back between the sinewy roots of the ancient cypress and gnawed on his last apple core. The Pearl River wasn't much more than a sluggish mud puddle creeping past him here, but he knew that somewhere up north it must be fast and deep and cold. He'd really like to see that. And somehow he had to find his father. He had to give some serious thought to just how he was going to do that.

Off to his left, in the meadow that surrounded the ferry landing, the shrieks of children playing drew his attention away from the dark water. Maybe that's what freedom was—being able to laugh and run around without anybody coming after you with a switch. Curious to see what all the commotion was about, he crawled out of his hideaway and made his way toward the edge of the cypress grove and the happy sounds.

A few folks had gathered around, sitting on the grass, enjoying the evening's lingering warmth. Standing downhill from them was a tall, clean-shaven white man, his feet planted firmly, and a book open in his hands. His dark hair looked like it hadn't been cut in a month of Sundays, and only then by some blind man with a straight razor, but it was neatly combed. He was as thin as a fence rail, and it looked like he'd pulled his clothes out of a trash heap somewhere, but as faded and stained as they were, the Reb uniform pants were unmistakeable. His strong, warm voice carried across the meadow as he tried to get the attention of the people scattered around. He wasn't having much luck, but he continued anyway, lines of stubborn determination creasing his tanned, even features. Tad shoved the remainder of the apple, core and all, into his mouth, licked the sweet nectar off his fingers, and settled onto his stomach in the weeds, ready for a little entertainment.

Sunday evening arrived, but the congregation didn't. The evening was still a bit warm and soft, and that's probably what attracted the two families with numerous small, energetic children along with the elderly couple out for a stroll. Eventually a young courting couple arrived and spread out a picnic blanket under an elm. All of these people may have habitually, for years, sat along the banks of the Pearl River on a Sunday evening for all Campbell knew. Regardless, he endeavored to deliver his carefully thought-out sermon, attempting to speak loud enough to be heard over the occasional squeals of the children. It did not seem to be received with the greatest spiritual affinity. In fact, Cam was not absolutely certain that it had been received at all, though once or twice he did think he established eye contact with the elderly gentleman. He chose to abbreviate this particular Sunday evening's message, its being his first one and all, so he pronounced the benediction. "May the Lord bless and keep you. May the Lord make His face to shine upon you and be gracious unto you. May the Lord lift up His Countenance unto you and give you peace. Amen."

The 'congregation', such as it was, began dispersing. The young parents herded their protesting children into a little flock and shooed them up the embankment. The elderly couple smiled politely at him as they passed. Maybe before Campbell came along to preach they had been accustomed to lingering a while longer along the river on a Sunday evening. Campbell didn't know. As he watched his 'flock' take flight, he began gathering up the songbooks which he had scattered around the area before anyone arrived. He thought that at least one or two members of the group might have picked one up, if for no other reason than out of curiosity. But, as it was, each book sat undisturbed precisely where Cam had placed it. Well, maybe he was a little responsible for that, he thought. After their passive response to his message, he had decided to omit the hymn-singing portion of the service this time.

As Cam continued collecting the books, scored only by the crickets' song and an occasional croak from a frog, all apparently equally unimpressed with his service, a young voice announced, "Shoot... you ain't no preacher."

Campbell turned in the direction of the pronouncement. From out of the shadows of some cypress trees sauntered a black boy about nine or ten years old. He planted himself decisively in front of Cam, looking up at him with bright black eyes and a quizzical smile. "You know why I say that?"

The boy was the personification of a ragamuffin, dressed in a worn homespun shirt and trousers that hung on his skinny frame, and his curly hair looked like it would need a good trimming soon. Cam held the boy's frank gaze for a moment, but he was in no mood to listen to a critique of his preaching skills from a child. Without answering, he turned and started toward his horse.

The boy, skipping along after him, persisted, "You wanna know why I say that?"

Campbell started packing the books into the saddlebags, finally responding, "Not particularly."

The boy volunteered, nevertheless. "Because you didn't take up no collection!"

Cam corrected the grammar. "Any... any collection."

"That's what I'm talkin' about. You didn't take up none!" the boy agreed.

Campbell muttered, half under his breath, "An offering...."

"What?"

This time, using more words, Campbell explained, "An offering. It's also called an offering. That's what I'm doing, offering, not collecting."

The boy screwed up his face in confusion. "How you live then?"

"Off the land. And the good graces of the people."

"What?"

"The land... off the land," Cam repeated.

The boy shook his head and scratched at a spot on his arm. "Massah Ed... he live off'n the land, too, exceptin' he sure live a whole heap better'n you. He up in that big brick house of his."

Cam cinched his saddlebags shut and turned to the boy. "Oh, and where might that be?"

"Ah, he dead now. Done went and got hisself kilt after them Yankees come through and burnt him out."

"Yeah. . . " Cam grunted as he mounted his horse.

Reaching up and grabbing the horse's bit, the boy squinted up at Campbell and asked, "Where you off to anyways, Preacherman?"

"The circuit." Cam settled into the saddle and gathered the reins.

"You gonna join up with the CIRCUS?" the boy exclaimed in unabashed excitement.

"Circuit, the preaching circuit," Campbell quickly corrected.

But the boy was already off and running in his youthful imagination. "Boy oh boy, I tell ya, one come through Cross Landin' one time. Man, I never seed such a thing!"

Cam chuckled but attempted to clarify. "I'm going to ride the circuit, spreading the word."

It was too late. The boy was already in the bigtop tents with the elephants and clowns. "You gonna ride in the circus, spreading the WHAT?" The boy laughed heartily at his own joke. When he got his laughter under control, he settled down. "What you called. . . really?"

"Campbell."

"And where you bound to anyways?"

"But I go by 'Cam'," Campbell elucidated on his last answer.

"On your way wheres?"

"I'm called 'Cam'," Campbell repeated.

"Alright. But where you going to. . . ?" The boy was growing impatient.

Campbell sighed, tiring of this verbal jousting. He adjusted himself in the saddle, and finally said, "You really are some-thing, you are, boy."

The boy's voice now softened a decibel. "I's free...is what I is."

Campbell wondered if a ten-year-old could truly under-stand the momentous nature of that simple statement. "And what are you going to do with your new freedom, son?"

The boy paused and lowered his head to eye his toe as he burrowed it into the earth for an answer. "I dunno. Same as everybody else, I reckon."

"Well, I do wish you a lot of luck, young fellow." Cam reined Annie around to leave.

Quickly, the boy reached up, grabbing the reins. "Wait! Don't you even wanna know who I am?"

Campbell reined back, steadying the roan, realizing his shortsightedness. "Well, please forgive me, my good man. Indeed, I would most surely like to know you."

The boy stood to his full height, squared his shoulders, and proudly announced, "My name is Tademus Co of Marion County, Mis'sippi!"

Campbell extended his arm to shake hands with Tademus Co. "Well, that's a mighty fine name indeed, Master Co, and a good place to be from, too, I reckon." Young Tademus' small, bony hand gripped his with surprising strength. "And I'm real proud to have made your acquaintance."

With that, Campbell reined Annie around and, this time, started riding away, calling back, "You take real good care of yourself now, you hear? And good luck to you!"

The horse quickly took her head. Tademus reached out to grab the reins again, but this time was too late.

Tad looked off after the preacherman for a few moments, watching him ride into the distance, then called out, "You ain't made my acquaintance yet!"

But the preacher was too far away by then to hear. Tad watched Campbell's diminishing figure until he was out of sight, then muttered to himself, "And you never did tell me wheres you was headin'. . . " But it was obviously north.

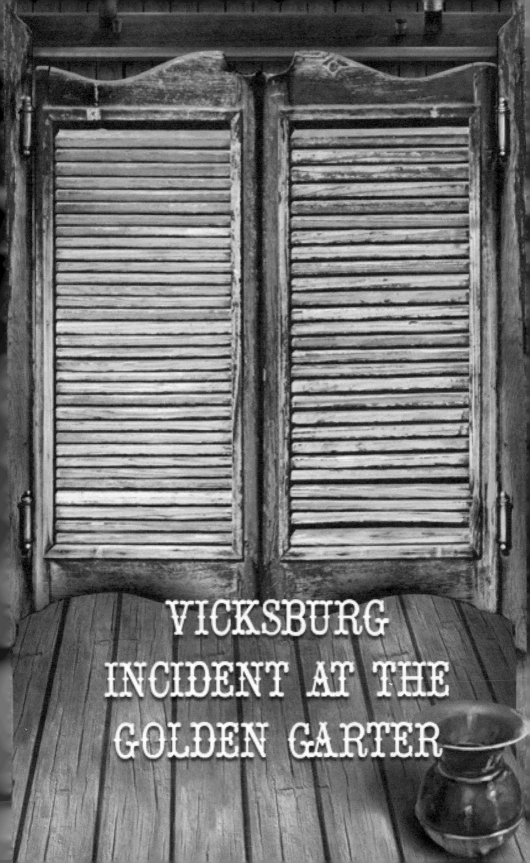

VICKSBURG
INCIDENT AT THE
GOLDEN GARTER

CHAPTER

4

"FIFTEEN DOLLARS?" Campbell exclaimed. He had no idea steamboat passage was going to be so expensive.

The Natchez Belle Steamboat's ticket agent blinked at him through thick glasses from the other side of the counter. "Yessiree. Space on the riverboats is at a premium these days, Mister, what with all the Yanks wanting to head home and all. And the Natchez Belle folks certainly ain't gonna pass up their chance at the profits. And then there was that terrible tragedy up near Memphis..." The little man shook his head.

Cam had read the newspaper accounts of the massive explosion and sinking of the Steamboat Sultana, as it headed north carrying thousands of homeward bound and war-weary soldiers a week or so ago. It gave him second thoughts about traveling by steamer, but it really was still the fastest way to St. Louis and then on to his ultimate destination. And he'd already said goodbye to faithful, patient Annie, and gotten a decent price for her and her tack at the Vicksburg livery.

The ticket agent was anxious to get to the paying customers lining up behind him. "So you wanna buy a ticket or not, Mister? That's fifteen dollars Federate, by the way. None of that worthless Confederate paper."

Deciding to hold onto his gold, Cam pulled out some of the wadded bills he'd gotten in payment for the horse, and handed the appropriate ones to the agent.

In return, the agent slid the ticket across the counter to him. "The boat leaves promptly at noon and don't wait for stragglers. Have a safe trip, son."

As Campbell walked away from the docks, heading up the hill into town, his stomach reminded him that breakfast was the next order of business. He had heard horror stories about the siege of Vicksburg back in '63, but the modest homes and shops he passed appeared to have survived the worst, and business was booming now, thanks to the town's strategic location on the Mighty Mississippi. The whole of the newly reunited country seemed to be on the move, passing directly through the bustling streets of Vicksburg.

The Golden Garter Saloon and Cafe was the first eating establishment he passed, and the smells wafting from within made it almost impossible for him to pass it by. On the other side of the massive stained-glass adorned oaken doors, Campbell entered a large room crowded with dozens of dining tables, each covered with a rich red table cloth. Most were already occupied by men breaking their fast with companions, smoking and discussing the affairs of the day. An ornately carved bar with brass fittings stretched the length of one wall, and behind it, an enormous mirror reached to the high ceiling, making the place seem even more imposing. Heavily flocked red wallpaper decorated the other walls, with windows draped in a lavish brocade which remained true to the color scheme. At the rear of the room, a wide, bold staircase led up to a balcony which looked down on the proceedings of the main floor. Judging by the decor, it was readily apparent to Cam that upstairs were the rooms let by the hour, accommodating the establishment's other lucrative post-war business. Perhaps this wasn't the best choice for a quiet breakfast, but Cam's stomach refused to let him leave.

He had just eased himself into the red velvet trimmed chair at an empty table near the bar when a young woman approached, smiling at him appreciatively. Although she was apparently the waitress, she was attired in bright royal blue, in stark contrast to the decor, tight around her slim waist and with a bodice cut lower than would be practical for someone serving hot meals. This was just her day job, Cam opined to himself. Her frank gaze made him suddenly aware of his dusty, oft-mended uniform trousers and stained shirt. Removing his battered Confederate cap, he quickly ran a hand through his mussed hair in an attempt at grooming.

"Can I do something for you, Soldier?" she purred, taking him in from head to toe, lingering briefly to assess his reflexive reaction to her invitation.

He had to make a concerted effort to pull his eyes away from her abundant endowments and find his voice. "Breakfast," he finally said, clearing his throat. "I'll have some breakfast, please."

The waitress's smiling gaze came back up to his eyes. "Well, you want to give it to me?" she teased, thoroughly enjoying her double entendre.

He returned her smile, appreciating her game—then shifted and straighten-up in his chair.

The big front door squeaked on its hinges as it pushed open, drawing his attention away from the blue-clad temptation in front of him. There, silhouetted by the morning sun, stood the spare figure of Tademus Co. The boy's eyes quickly took in the whole room and lit up with glee when he spotted Cam. With an enthusiastic wave, he bounced his way among the tables and came to plop into the empty chair across from Campbell, as if he'd been expected. "Mornin', Preacher! You ordered yet?"

Cam raised a questioning eyebrow at his new dining companion, then turned to the waitress. "Some eggs and biscuits, please. And coffee. For both of us."

The smile faded from the girl's face as she huffed away from the table.

"Don't you want no meat?" Tad challenged. "I always have me some kinda meat for my breakfast."

"That is for a fact, you say?"

But the boy's attention had flitted elsewhere, as he watched the waitress go about her work. "Boy, she is some kinda purdy ain't she? I seen the way you was eyeballing her...a shameful way for a preacherman to be looking at a woman, I'd say."

Cam leaned back in his chair, watching the child in front of him as Tad studied the room, taking in every detail. He was still dressed in the ragged clothes Cam had first seen him in, but looked none the worse for wear for having made his way all the way from Sandy Hook.

Having finished his survey of the saloon, Tad elected to fill the silence. "I reckon as how you ain't much for preaching this morning, huh? Or talking neither, for that matter. What's the matter, ain't you pleased to see me?"

"Yeah, I'm glad to see you. I just wasn't expecting you. How did you get here?"

"By the good graces of the peoples," Tad grinned, exceedingly proud of himself for throwing back Cam's exact words from days earlier. "Lots of nice folks along the roads these days, traveling to get someplace better. Some didn't mind giving me a ride, and I didn't mind helping them out with chores and work and things like that."

"Very resourceful."

"Very what?"

Campbell chuckled. "It's very smart of you to barter work for your passage north."

Tad got even more excited. "And looky here at this." He pulled a folded piece of paper from inside his shirt and handed it across the table.

Cam unfolded the flyer and turned it right side up. At the top was a drawing of a paddle wheel steamer. Beneath, in bold type, it read:

FOR HIRE-Cabin Boy-Natchez Belle Steamboat Line
quarters, board, and twenty-five cents a day
Inquire-Ticket Office

"I got the man to read it for me," Tad explained. "And I already got me the job. The boat leaves at twelve o'clock sharp."

Campbell was puzzled, so he had to ask. "Why are you headed north? You wouldn't by any chance be trailing me, would you?"

Tad frowned and shook his head emphatically. "What, me coming 'round after you? Shoot, man, I ain't even studying about you. I just gotta get me some eats before I catch me the steamer to St. Louie."

Campbell opened his mouth to pursue this further, but was interrupted by the waitress' return. She set a plate of scrambled eggs, a plate of biscuits, and a cup of coffee on the table in front of Campbell.

"We need another plate," Cam observed.

The girl wiped her hands nervously on her towel. "Listen, Mister, don't cause no stir. You know I can't serve him in here." Then she hurriedly walked away.

Campbell drew in a breath and let it out with a huff. Things certainly aren't going to change overnight, he mused as he dumped the biscuits onto the table and served a portion of eggs onto the emptied platter. He set it down in front of Tad, who seemed not to notice the waitress's curt attitude. He'd already reached over and helped himself to Campbell's spoon. Through a mouthful of eggs, he mumbled, "Pass the biscuits, please, Preacherman."

Campbell picked up one of the warm pieces of bread and dropped it on Tad's plate.

Just as Cam was about to dig into his own breakfast, he was interrupted by two other patrons of the saloon who paused at his table on their way out. He'd seen them at a back table when he'd first come in, and by their dress and demeanor, he'd judged them to be local business leaders discussing a profitable deal over breakfast.

"Permit me, Sir," spoke the first man. "Jenkins is my name."

"Campbell McCool," Cam replied, leaning forward.

Jenkins gestured to his companion, continuing the introductions, "My associate, Mr. Kemp."

Kemp stood behind Jenkins, away from the table, his arms tightly crossed, a deep frown hidden behind his mustache.

"We must presume you to be a traveling man," Jenkins began, "just passing on through our fair city, and we, by no means, would have you feel unwelcome. However, this cafe here is one of your more respectable establishments, and there are codes of ethics by which we do endeavor to conduct ourselves. I'm sure you'll understand and abide accordingly." He grimaced in Tad's direction, clearly transmitting his point, then added, "As a gentleman, that is."

"As a gentleman, of course," Cam repeated, eyes narrowing.

Jenkins continued. "Why, yessir. I can see by your colors that you did, after all, fight the good fight, and we citizens certainly want all our boys to know that their gallant efforts on the battlefields were, in no way, waged in vain. Declarations of peace, by no measure or means, constitute an end to the grand traditions of the South. Those, we do intend to uphold "

"A proud man you are indeed, Mr Jenkins," Campbell responded, mustering as much gravity as possible to mask his rising anger.

"Thank you, sir." Jenkins nodded and smiled, and turned for the door. But Kemp picked up Tad's plate of eggs and set it down on the bar on his way out.

"I wasn't near about finished!" Tad complained.

Campbell watched the two buffoons as they exited, chuckling smugly to themselves. Again, he huffed a sigh, pushed back from the table, and walked over to the bar to retrieve the plate of eggs. Returning and setting the plate back down on the table before Tad, he quietly suggested, "Well, suppose we both finish, and then let's just ease on outta here."

As Tad plowed back into his eggs, two more of the saloon's patrons swaggered up to their table, to continue where Jenkins and Kemp left off. The heavy one, in the red checked shirt, was the spokesman this time. "I believe you need to hear it again, spoke more plain-like. This here 'boy' can take his grub out back, yonder, by the smokehouse. There's a table all set up there and everything for his kind."

Cam tightened his fists, feeling his annoyance bubble up to the level of anger again. "And what kind might his be, friend?"

The other man, the quiet one with the ugly scar, stared Campbell in the eye, his lips tightening. Then suddenly he reached down, grabbing Cam by the shirt front, and lifted him abruptly from the table, knocking over the chair in the process. "Talking's all finished, Mister."

Cam threw up his arms, breaking the man's grasp, then shoved him away hard. He slammed backward into the bar, sending glassware flying. Red Shirt intervened, throwing a wide right. Campbell easily blocked it and returned with two quick jabs to the man's stomach, doubling him over. A solid uppercut connected with jaw bone, sending Red Shirt sprawling into a neighboring table.

Before Cam could even straighten, he knew Scarface was behind him. The sudden hard blow sent a lightening bolt of pain shattering into white-hot stars in his brain, and he fell into total blackness.

Black faded into gray. The pulsing in his head quickly turned to pain, then other sensations emerged—rough wood under his hands, the smell of horse manure, charred wood, and cooked eggs. His stomach threatened to reject its contents, and he drew in slow, deep breaths to tame it. When he felt enough in control, he dared to open his eyes and move a hand. He discovered himself to be sitting, leaning on an unsteady plank table, his head resting on his arms. He was outside, in the warm sunlight, and the burnt wood smell was coming from the listing, dilapidated smoke house to his right. Tad sat across from him, busily finishing his breakfast.

Not daring to lift his head, fearing another wave of nausea, Cam muttered, "No offense meant, Tad, but I just don't see how this is going to work out."

Tad swallowed a mouthful of eggs and bit into a biscuit. "You was looking pretty good in there, Preacher. I'd've jumped right in and helped you out, onlys I was sure you could handle just them twos."

Taking a breath to steady himself, Cam slowly sat up as straight as his head would allow him. "Tad...do you hear what I'm saying?"

"Sure, I hear'd ya." Tad wiped the last morsel of food off his plate with a piece of biscuit, then eyed the plate of untouched eggs sitting in front of Campbell.

Campbell slid the plate across to him.

With spoon poised, Tad afforded Cam one last chance to change his mind. "You sure?"

Campbell nodded, the pain bouncing off the inside of his skull. He'd held his head off the table about as long as he could for right now, so he eased it back down to rest on his arms just a little while longer. As the fog cleared, and coherent thought returned, he wondered what time it was, and remembered the paddle wheel steamboat that would be departing the dock exactly at noon, no later. That's precisely where he and Tad would be...together.

THE NATCHEZ BELLE

CHAPTER
5

THE NATCHEZ BELLE STEAMBOAT COMPANY did not seem to have taken a lesson from the deadly disaster that had been the fiery sinking of the Sultana. The newspaper accounts said hundreds had lost their lives that night because the boat had been overloaded with soldiers making their way home after the truce had been announced. However if there were soldiers still eager to get back north, and money to be made, then the Natchez Belle would sell tickets to as many souls as she could fit onto her decks. Despite his pounding head, Campbell had boarded early enough to secure a patch of deck on the leeward side of an upper level, just aft of the bow. He'd spread his bedroll out on the deck next to the bulkhead and settled into what would be his home for the next several weeks, as the Natchez Belle wound her way northward toward St. Louis.

Strewn around him on this deck, and all the others, were soldiers and sailors from both sides, staking out their own little corner for the long trip home. Just down the deck to his right, a Yankee private who introduced himself as Henry had laid out his own worn blanket. If he took notice at all of the remains of Cam's Confederate uniform, it didn't seem to make any difference to him. Around the corner to his left, facing the on-coming wind from the bow, was an emaciated young man dressed in what could only be described as rags, who said his name was Walter. After he explained that he was recently released from Andersonville Prison, he curled up into himself and said nothing else. Cam had offered to trade places with him, so he wouldn't be sitting directly in the wind, but the boy just shook his head and refused to move.

The other passengers of the Natchez Belle reflected a cross-section of post-Civil War humanity. There were gamblers and sundry other soldiers of fortune, businessmen, merchants, farmers, politicians, carpetbaggers, and cabaret entertainers from the French quarters of New Orleans. The wealthier or more influential enjoyed the luxury of the private cabins. And ladies of questionable reputation subtly offered their services to whomever might produce the price for human closeness. Several correspondents and artists, likewise, were on board, still busily writing and drawing their reports to furnish the readers of "Harper's Weekly" an on-going first hand account of the aftermath of destruction.

On his first couple of nights on board, fighting a lingering headache and unable to settle his thoughts, Cam had sought out the grand salon on the main deck and, with some of what he'd earned from the sale of Annie, bought his way into one of the card games. He was no greenhorn. While in medical school, he'd earned a reputation as a shrewd poker player, and he quickly sized up his table of opponents. Three were Yankee infantrymen, and the dealer, though conservatively dressed as a businessman, handled the deck with a little too much ease and confidence to fool Cam. When Cam began to win, he was sorely tempted to continue playing and prolong that singular elation of victory. But he knew the card shark was merely softening him up for a big kill, so he took his winnings and left the other three to their certain fate. A petite redhead in a strategically revealing gown offered to relieve him of some of his winnings, and though he gave it a passing thought, he decided to skip that temptation too, at least for a while.

After years of war and the particular horrors of the last several months, Campbell found that just sitting on the deck and watching the banks of the Mighty Mississippi roll by was a balm to his mind and his soul. The special new green of spring flowed by endlessly, occasionally disrupted by a freshly turned field, or a pasture grazing a few cows. White-washed houses peeked out from stands of oak and birch high on cliffs overlooking the river. Even the drone of the boilers and the churning of the paddle wheels came to lull him in his sleeping and waking hours.

When he wasn't lost in the scenery, Cam pulled out the tintype he'd taken from Marler, the boy he had killed on that fateful final day of fighting. He had come to feel that he already knew the people pictured there. Seated in a solid, straight-backed chair, stern and patriarchal, was a man looking to be in his 50's, dressed in his Sunday best, sporting neatly trimmed mutton chops. In a more ornate chair, upholstered in a bold flower print, was his wife, a spare woman attired in a dark dress trimmed in white lace, with the wide skirt that was the fashion of the day. Although she didn't smile, there was something about her face, and the way her hands were folded in her lap, that made Cam believe she was warm and nurturing, the kind who welcomed and cared for all. Next to her stood a girl of about twelve, who was trying hard not to smile, even though her dimples gave her away. She was dressed similar to her mother, but even in the tiny tintype, Cam could see the mischievous spark in her eyes. Marler stood straight and tall behind his father, in a suit that was just a little too small. One hand rested on the back of his father's chair, and the other was formally tucked inside his suit jacket. He wanted very much to look older than he was.

Cam had studied the neat printing on the back of the tintype until he'd memorized it. "The Manning Family - Jefferson City, Missouri - 1861". Once he'd made his way to Jefferson

City, Cam knew it wouldn't be difficult to track down the Mannings. If he let himself conjure that meeting in his imagination, it was a moment he both yearned for and dreaded.

When he'd wander the decks for a change of scenery and to stretch his legs, or in the dining room at mealtime, he'd catch a glimpse of Tad's rushing about through the crowds, dressed in his fancy new cabin boy's uniform, complete with a gold-trimmed "captain's" cap. The boy was definitely earning his 25¢ a day. On their third night on the river, Cam was standing in line waiting to pick up his dinner when he was distracted from a conversation with the young couple in front of him. A commotion had broken out in the main dining room where the cabin passengers sat at linen-draped tables and ate with fine silverware. Through the gilded archway to his left, he could see a portly older man practically turning purple in his anger. When the crowd shifted, Cam saw that the old man was gripping Tad tightly by the stiff white collar of his new uniform, lifting the terrified boy off of his feet and shaking him violently. Words like "clumsy" and "ignorant" and "darkie" spewed from him like lava.

Cam barreled through the crowd and to the man's table, where he looped an arm around Tad's skinny waist and wrenched the man's grip from the boy's shirt front. Tad quickly scurried behind him.

"You will not speak to the boy in that manner, friend," Cam growled.

Startled, the man blinked and stepped back, but quickly found his voice. "I will speak to this uncivilized little pickaninny any way I wish, sir. If he is your property, I suggest you keep him properly constrained."

"He is no one's property, mister." Cam was aware that everyone in the room had gone quiet, staring at him. He reached behind him and pulled Tad to his side, putting an arm around his slender shoulders. "He's a paid employee on this steamboat. If you have a quarrel with how he does his job, I suggest you take it up with the Captain. Or else you can take it up with me."

Again the old man blinked in disbelief, and anxiously surveyed the room seeking support. He found none, as the other diners chose to return to their meals. Finally he harrumphed and straightened his jacket. "Yes, the Captain will definitely hear from me about this incident. The child will need to be heartily reprimanded."

Cam glared at him, his fists balled so tightly his nails dug into his palms, until the old man's eyes darted away, and he retook his seat as if nothing had happened.

"Come on, let's go," Cam whispered as he guided Tad towards the main entrance and out into the passageway.

"It weren't my fault, Preacher," Tad protested. "He the one who spilt his own glass. I weren't anywheres near it."

"It's okay, Tad." Cam felt his heart pounding, realizing what he had just done without the hint of a second thought. "Why don't you and I go have a chat with the Captain before your friend in there has a chance to."

The Captain had been surprisingly understanding when Cam had explained the incident. Apparently he'd had similar experiences with the same passenger. And Tad had been surprisingly restrained. There were probably similar instances in the boy's past, Cam thought, when he'd learned that keeping his natural exuberance subdued was in his own best interests. Following their visit with the Captain, they'd both returned to Cam's little niche on the upper deck and settled onto the bedroll. From his saddlebag, Cam pulled out a cookie he'd saved from dinner the night before and handed it to Tad.

As if he'd already forgotten all about the fracas in the salon, Tad mumbled around a mouthful of cookie, "I sure hope you ain't gonna start up a preachin' on this here boat! You ain't, is ya?"

Cam smiled. "I've been working on a sermon..."

"If you gonna be a preacher, what you first gotta do is look like a preacher and get shut of them soldier pants of your'n." Tad pulled at the cuffs of his starched black jacket and adjusted his bow tie. "What you gotta do is get you a black suit kinda like mine, onlys you can't wear no cap like this one, 'a course."

Campbell lifted the cap from Tad's head, brushed some dust from its crown, then set it back, adjusting it just right. "And once you get to St. Louis, Cabin Boy Tademus, what happens with this new career?"

"I's setting out for my Pa, then, that's what. He up north."

"Yeah, well that could mean a lot of places other than St. Louis," Cam pointed out.

"He got took in by some Union troops what had some 'coloreds' in it and wearing blue uniforms, and Massah Ed he say they be outta Missoura."

"You're telling me that your Pa just up and left with these Federate troops?" Cam had heard that many slaves who had escaped or who were left to their own resources when their masters were killed, had been welcomed into Yankee regiments.

"I's saying he got took in, and I's aiming to catch up to him—and I will, too, some day."

"You got no other folks anywhere?"

Tad finished the last of the cookie and stared out across the dark water to the darker shoreline. "My Ma, she dead now not more than a year back."

"I'm sorry, Tad." Cam placed a hand on the boy's shoulder, but he didn't seem to notice. "But you'll locate your Pa soon, I'm sure."

Tad recovered quickly, and a smile lit up his face. "I sure will." He popped to his feet and gave Cam a curt little salute. "Well, I gotta gets me back to work now. You promise you ain't gonna start preaching or nothing?"

Cam returned the salute. "I guess not, until I'm attired in the proper clothes for the job, like you are."

"That's good." Tad breathed a sigh of relief, and hurried off, bounding down the stairwell.

THE SEARCH BEGINS

CHAPTER

6

IT WAS MIDDAY as the Natchez Belle entered the port of St. Louis and began maneuvering her way in to dock. Careening her side against the landing as gangplanks were thrust ashore along with ropes for tying down, the Belle belched one last bellow of black smoke from her stacks and, with a final blast from her horns, announced her arrival, the paddlewheel thrashing to a halt. Passengers began hurriedly disembarking against the flow of new, now boarding, passengers, the throngs swirling with determination and purpose.

Leaning on the railing of his upper deck, Cam watched and waited for the stampede to abate. Following the long, dark night of war, all the towns and cities they'd visited during their voyage up river seemed to be bursting with new life and an eagerness to begin rebuilding. After all, there was money to be made, Cam mused, smiling at his own cynicism.

As the crowds thinned, Cam gathered up his bedroll, threw the saddlebags over his shoulder, and turned to head for the gangplank. Then he heard the unmistakable shout. "Preacher! Preacher! Hold up!" Tad skidded to a halt in front of him, out of breath. "You wasn't about to leave without saying good-bye, was ya?"

"Oh, not a chance of that." Cam patted Tad firmly on the shoulder. "I just didn't want to be in the way while you were disappointing the Natchez Belle Captain with your resignation."

Having relinquished his cabin boy's uniform, Tad had returned to the thread-bare homespun he'd been wearing the day they'd first met. There was a new tear in the right elbow, and the pants were a bit short. Cam looked out toward the main street leading up the hill into the bustling city and came to a decision. "The fact of the matter is, I thought I'd hang around for a while and maybe help you find Army Headquarters. They might be able to put you on the right track toward locating your Pa."

Tad's eyes lit up like Christmas candles, but he quickly schooled his face into a serious frown. "Yeah, well, that's what I was aiming to do myself. But you kin come along, if'n you wanna."

"Thank you. I think I'd like that." Cam put his arm around Tad's shoulders and guided him toward the ladder down to the lower deck. "But now that you've resigned your commission, I think the first order of business is to find you some suitable civilian duds."

The street leading up the hill away from the dock was lined with shops and cafes, all doing a land-office business with the quickly growing trade along the river. They'd only walked a couple of blocks when they came upon a general store that had various useful goods displayed in its front window, including men's and boys' work clothes. When Cam pushed open the front door, a small bell tinkled cheerily. He motioned for Tad to enter, but the boy held back.

"It's alright," Cam urged quietly. "Go on in."

The lanky shop keeper, his glasses perched securely atop his bald head, looked up from his dusting, beaming with a welcoming smile, which quickly disappeared. But he spoke cordially enough. "Good day to you, Soldier. How may I serve you?"

Stepping over to a shelf of folded shirts, Cam picked one up, shook it out, and held it up to Tad, checking the size. "We're in the market for some new clothes for this young man."

The shop keeper bustled over and snatched the shirt away, as if he were afraid it might touch Tad. His uneasy smile returned. "I'd be pleased to sell you a stylish replacement for your...uniform..., sir. However, there are other, more appropriate establishments for the darkie to find what he wants."

Cam took a deep breath. He was really getting tired of this. He politely took back the shirt. "But we like this one. Right, Tad?"

Tad silently nodded.

"And some trousers, as well," Cam added, picking up a pair from a lower shelf, once again holding them up to Tad's waist to judge the fit.

"Sir, I must insist...."

"Insist what, friend?" Cam pulled his leather pouch from his pocket and extracted one of the smaller gold coins, then looked the shopkeeper directly in the eye. "That you're not interested in taking my money?"

The merchant practically salivated at the sight of gold, and stammered, "I would most happily sell you anything..."

"Good. That seals it, then." Cam took the man's bony hand and pressed the coin into it. "We'll take the shirt and the trousers. No need to wrap them." As he pushed Tad toward the door, he spoke loud enough for the shopkeeper to hear. "Let's go, Tad. We have a lot more shopping to do, but I don't think this merchant has anything else we need."

The little bell over the door jingled musically as they left.

The very first person they asked was able to direct them to the U.S. Army Headquarters, which now occupied the second floor of the county courthouse. It was a gleaming monster of a marble building topped by a massive dome, the likes of which Cam hadn't seen since his time in Atlanta. From the size of Tad's eyes as they entered the cavernous rotunda, embellished with colorful murals, it was apparent that the boy had never seen anything like it in his life.

"This here's like a castle or something," the boy breathed, sticking close at Cam's side. "Who lives here?"

"No one lives here," Cam explained. "This is where the business of the state and county is conducted, and where court is held."

Tad just nodded, trying to take in all the grandeur at once.

The sergeant seated at an imposing mahogany desk on the far side of the rotunda looked up from his paper work long enough to direct them up the wide staircase to their right, and along the curving hallway that overlooked the main floor below. Tad approached the railing to glance down, but quickly returned to Cam's side.

Behind the heavy oak door marked "U. S. Army" was a large room crowded with desks and men in uniform, none of whom even glanced up as they entered. They approached the Captain sitting at the nearest desk, and Cam introduced himself and repeated his request.

"Our Negro units had really increased by the time of the surrender, Mr. McCool," the Captain told them. "I could provide you with a list of the black regiments we have on file, but I'm afraid you'll find our records far from complete."

"We'd be obliged for any information you might be able to give us."

The captain got up from his desk and walked over to a bank of four wooden, four-drawer filing cabinets. He searched among them for several minutes, gathering some ledgers, then he carried the books over and set them down on a wide counter fronting the room. Cam and Tad followed.

"You must understand that the blacks made for pretty easy recruits, generally speaking, and their numbers were really growing toward the last," the Captain explained. "You're welcome to go over these ledgers if you'd like, Mr. McCool.

Most of them were compiled from commanders' field reports. They're listed according to campaigns, in order that some record could be kept of body counts, casualties, recruits and so forth. You see here...look..."

The Captain opened one of the ledgers and pointed to a page crowded with names, dates and numbers, all scribbled in various hands, some legible, others not so much so. "Our Negro units you'll find listed separately at the bottom of the various columns." He turned the page. "Then here's a whole page full of them. Like I say, they were coming by the droves before the final cannon blast. I wish you boys luck."

The captain dismissed himself and returned to his overflowing desk. Campbell reached across the counter for pencil and paper and began taking notes.

Cam left the Courthouse with a pocket bulging with notes and the growing dread that this might be an impossible task. But he made an effort to remain positive, for Tad's sake. The boy was alone in the world and truly needed to find his father. First there were some necessities to take care of, though. In this booming river town economy, he had to do some tough haggling to secure suitable horses and gear at a price he could afford. Tad had insisted on throwing his hard earned wages into the pot, and they stocked up on a few staples, like flour and coffee. Then they began their search in earnest.

After four days of tracking down and talking to soldiers and veterans alike, they got their first substantial lead, which took them to an encampment area just outside of St. Louis. Muddy from the recent rain, and smelling of manure, camp fires, and unwashed bodies, it conjured for Cam the nightmarish memories of those final months on the battlefield.

He had to remind himself that his time in such places was behind him, and he focused on the mission at hand.

A harried young corporal pointed out the large tent on the outskirts of the bivouac. A private standing guard outside announced their arrival to the commanding general, a lean, angular man looking much too young for the rank, who was busy at his field desk inside.

They were invited to sit, and Campbell explained their search, ending with the sparse information he'd gleaned from the Army records. "I figure him to have joined up, possibly with General Canby's forces down around Mobile and Fort Blakely."

"Well, that could have been Colonel Geddes' Third Division." The officer stretched out his legs and leaned back in his chair, tapping the end of his pen against the desk top. "It was, however, a very large command, with many divisional brigades. You might check, though, with a Lieutenant Reichter, Bard Reichter. I know Reichter wasn't with Banks, but it seems to me I've heard him talking about Admiral Porter, and some bayou efforts made in conjunction with the Navy down around those parts. I don't know if he can be of any help."

The general told Campbell and Tad where he thought they might find Lieutenant Reichter, and it had taken them another two days to locate his small dirt farm near the town of Washington, on the Missouri River. About all they were able to learn from Reichter was that a Brigadier General named Alcus Smith had led a brigade under Major General Canby in that vicinity that Reichter recalled had some Negroes among the ranks. But as to where they might track down Smith, he could only guess. Reichter thought he was from somewhere in the middle of the state. Campbell thanked him kindly, and they rode away with yet another impossible task standing in the way of their goal—search the entire heart of Missouri for a man named Smith.

Night had fallen on their fourteenth consecutive day of this fruitless quest. This night was like all the others that had made up the last couple of weeks. They'd set up camp in a clearing near the river and silently eaten a sparse meal made from their dwindling supplies, yet again meatless.

The fire was burning low. The last of the evening's coffee had boiled away in the pan that sat close to the embers. Tad sat still and unusually quiet, gazing forlornly into the glowing embers. Across from him, Campbell read aloud from the Bible. "For I am the Way, the Truth, and the Light. No man shall enter the Kingdom of Heaven but by Me. . . ." Campbell glanced up at Tad, who was sitting with his legs crossed and his head down.

Campbell turned the pages of his Bible to other Scriptures and continued reading aloud. "God is our refuge and strength, a very present help in time of trouble."

He stole another look at Tad, but there was still no response.

Flipping through the book, Cam selected another verse. "He maketh wars to cease unto the end of the earth, he breaketh the bow, and cutteth the spear in sunder; he burneth the chariot in the fire. Be still and know I am God, the Lord of hosts is with us. Great is the Lord."

"You preaching at me?" Tad snapped.

So the boy was listening. "No, not just you," Cam answered. "To both of us, I suppose. . . " He let the silence hang in the warm evening air, watching Tad closely.

Finally, Tad picked up a piece of kindling and heaved it into the fire. "It say anything in there about how we gonna find my Pa?"

Without bowing his head or closing his eyes, keeping his eyes on the troubled young man highlighted in the glow of the dying fire, Campbell offered a prayer. "May You lead and guide us, oh Lord, on a true path so that we may reunite Tademus, here, with his Pa, if this be Thy will. Amen."

Tad kicked at the charred wood. "What you mean, 'if this be His will'? Why should it matter none to Him, anyways?"

"We all matter to Him, Tad, and everything we do also matters to Him. It's not for us to know, one way or another, just what God might intend for our lives. We just must hope that His will be done."

"Yeah, well what if'n the Lawd don't want me to find my Pa? Just where we gonna be then, you tell me?"

"Faith, Tad. We just have to have faith."

Picking up another piece of kindling, Tad scratched aimlessly in the dirt. A log popped and spit embers, and somewhere in the surrounding darkness a fox barked.

Still drawing swirls in the dirt, Tad finally asked, "You have to go to school to learn how to be a preacher?"

"Well, I never did, but then I'm not what you could rightfully call a real preacher," Cam explained. "But my Pa, though, he was in the seminary when I was born."

Tad's head came up, his eyes wide. "You was born in a GRAVEYARD?"

"Seminary, not cemetery," Cam tried to clarify. "A seminary is a school for theologians, for preachers."

"I sure never knowed you had to go to school to learn how to be no gravedigger."

Campbell huffed a frustrated sigh. Maybe now was a good time for some schooling. He scooted around the fire until he was sitting next to Tad, and he took the stick of kindling from his hand. "Here, let me show you something." Cam smoothed out the dirt where Tad had been doodling and with the point of the stick, he drew a T. "You know what that is?"

"Sure," Tad answered confidently. "That's a cross, like what's in a graveyard."

"Well, yeah, but it's also a 'tee', which is the first letter of your name."

Again Campbell put the tip of the stick to the ground and furrowed out, next to the T, first an A, then a D. "There, that spells your name—Tad." Then Cam called out each letter as he pointed to it. "T-A-D—Tad."

Smoothing out another patch of dirt, Cam wrote a C and an O, then explained, "C-O—Co. Tad Co. That's a picture of your name."

Tad squirmed to get a better look. "Draw me out 'preacher'," he insisted.

Once again, Campbell put the stick to work, shaping letters clearly, and calling off each as he drew it. "P-R-E-A-C-H-E-R."

Tad threw his head back and laughed out loud, sending the sweet sound echoing out into the night. "Yep, you a preacher, alright enough!"

Tad's laughter was contagious, and Cam couldn't help but join in. He hadn't laughed like this in weeks. Finally, he grabbed Tad's bedroll and spread it out on the ground next to the writing lesson. "Time to turn in, Mr. Co. We have a long ride tomorrow."

As Tad curled up in his blanket, Cam eased another dry log into the fire, to sustain its warmth for a while longer, and opened his Bible to John 7:16, "Jesus answered them, 'My teaching is not mine, but His who sent me.'"

Each morning Cam had made it customary that they set aside a few minutes for devotion. However, he woke the next morning to find that Tad had apparently been up and going for some time. The fire was already rekindled and fresh coffee was simmering.

Having rolled up his bedroll, Tad was sitting fireside, grinning like the cat that ate the canary. "Morning, Preacher! You planning on just laying there in that bedroll all day till cobwebs form, or we gonna get on?"

Campbell propped himself onto an elbow and looked over to where their horses were tied, grazing at their breakfast, and teased, "Why, you don't even have the horses saddled yet."

Tad grinned and tossed a stick at him.

After a quick breakfast of oatmeal, they broke camp, leaving a scorched patch marring the topsoil where their fire had been. When the horses were saddled and bridled, Campbell threw his bedroll behind the cantle and tied it down. Then he reached down for his saddlebags. As he slung them across the horse's rump, he stopped in mid-motion. There, freshly branded into the leather, in crude, large, but clearly legible letters stretching across the entire width of his saddlebags, was PREACHER - CO.

Something unfamiliar swelled in his chest and caught in his throat. There it was, permanently etched, for all to see. He turned to look into the young black face of Tademus Co of Marion County, Mississippi, now grinning back at him with shining pride.

CAM AND TAD BECOME
PREACHER AND CO

CHAPTER

7

SOMETIMES THEY RODE IN SILENCE, each lost in his own thoughts. The sun was getting higher and warmer each day, and it was all Cam could do to keep from dozing off in the saddle, lulled by the mare's gentle swaying gait. But often they passed the time talking. Or at least Tad did. When he had a story to tell, he could make it last for miles, filling in with colorful embellishments of life on Massah Ed's plantation. And they'd sing. Cam would start off with one of his favorite hymns and teach Tad the chorus so he could join in. But Tad's favorites were the spirituals he'd sung with his family and the other slaves. They were rousing and moving and heart-rending, and Tad bellowed them out with all the enthusiasm of a tent revival preacher, in a voice that would probably mature into a rich baritone one day. Cam enjoyed just listening as well as singing along.

Late on a particularly hot Wednesday morning, they found themselves at the ferry dock on the Missouri River near Boonville, waiting in the shade of an ancient elm for the ferry to return from its last crossing. One of the other travelers advised them that it shouldn't be more than hour's wait. As he'd done with every peddler and farmer and journeyman they'd passed on the road, Cam inquired of the half dozen others awaiting the ferry if they knew of an Alcus Smith, who supposedly resided in the region. And as had been the case with all the others, everyone just shook their head. So while the horses browsed nearby, Cam and Tad settled into the coolest spot they could find and nibbled on left-over oat cakes that Tad had fried up for breakfast that morning.

Cam finished chewing the last of his oat cake, brushed the crumbs off his hands, and pulled the small slate and piece of chalk out of his saddlebag. He'd realized that if Tad were ever to be able to read the Bible, he'd need to learn to read first, and that the evenings around their campfire were the perfect place to begin, so he'd splurged on the slate and chalk as a more suitable replacement for dirt and a stick.

Tad's eyes brightened at the sight of the slate. The boy had a quick and curious mind and was intrigued with how marks on the slate or a piece of paper could represent sounds and words. He scooted over next to Cam. "Draw me a picture of 'horse'," he insisted.

"I'll write the word for 'horse'," Cam corrected as he scratched out H-O-R-S-E on the slate, pronouncing the letters as he wrote them. Then he tapped at the S. "Remember how we talked about the S and how it stands for the hissing sounds in words."

Squinting up his eyes, Tad studied the word, then sounded it out slowly. "Horsey"

"No, just 'horse', not 'horsey.'"

"But it got that E hanging off the end there. That makes it 'horsey'."

Cam sighed. Several lessons in, and this was already getting more complicated than he knew how to handle. "Well, in this case, the E is silent. You don't pronounce it."

"Well, then why's it there?"

"It just is."

"That ain't no reason."

Since Cam couldn't come up with a good reason, he decided to take another path. "Okay, let's try another word.

Your horse is named Alice. We can write that out, too." With his shirt sleeve he wiped off 'horse' and printed A-L-I-C-E.

Tad cocked his head. "Where's the S?"

"Alice doesn't have an S in it."

"Sure it do. Al-iiissss," Tad hissed, drawing out the sound.

"Well, in this case, no...."

Shaking his head in frustration, Tad fell back into the grass. "There's 30-hundred different rules to this readin' and writin' mess. How's a body suppose to remember them all?'

"It is confusing at first," Cam admitted, making a mental note to start arithmetic lessons, too. "But you'll catch on. We'll work on it later. The ferry should be here soon."

Cam lay back in the cool grass, too, picking a stem and biting into its green sweetness. "Where'd you learn to make such good oat cakes?"

"My Ma was a kitchen slave," Tad told him matter-of-factly. "When I's little, she used to let me help. 'Til I's big enough to work in the fields." Tad giggled to himself, a sure sign he was warming up for another one of his stories. "I remember one time she's making Massah Ed's breakfast, frying up the best-smelling bacon, and I ain't had no breakfast yet, so I reached up to try to get me some, and my arm hit that stove..." Tad squealed with the memory. "Man, that was the day I learnt the meaning of the word 'hot'. See, I still gots the scar." Tad pulled back his right sleeve to show Cam the puckered, pink welt just below his palm. "I got me some whooping, too, and Mammy June—she the one that run the kitchen—she yelled, 'Alice, you get that li'l pickaninny outta this here kitchen afore he kills hisself and eats all Massah's breakfast!'"

Cam grinned. "You named your horse after your mother? That's sweet."

There was a brief silence, then Tad sat up. "I gots to remember her somehow...."

"So how'd you get that scar on your chin? Another kitchen mishap?"

Absently, Tad's hand went to the pale little mark along his jaw. It wasn't as prominent as the burn on his wrist, but it still must've hurt when it happened. Tad turned his gaze out across the slow, muddy river. "Naw, that was another fracas...."

Then the barriers came up. Cam had come to recognize the hooded eyes and the distant stare when they'd broached a subject Tad didn't want to talk about. It did't happen often, but Cam had learned to respect it when it did.

When the rest of the waiting passengers stirred to gather their belongings, Cam looked up to see the ferry approaching the dock, ladened with still more travelers, horses and goods. He gave Tad a gentle nudge, and they rose to collect the horses and join the queue for their turn to board.

Once the sturdy little ferry had finished loading its next contingent of pilgrims, and the vessel was underway, Cam approached the captain who looked like he'd been around a while and seen a lot. He chewed on a wad of tobacco and wore the cap of a sailor, though not one from this most recent war. He asked the old tar the same question he'd been asking everyone for days.

"Why that old redneck horse thief!" Yes, it was clear this old salt had had the pleasure of an acquaintance with Alcus Smith, or, at the very least, had heard of him. The captain spat dark tobacco juice into the water. "Alcus Smith's been trading the short stick for the long around Pettis County since he was old enough to wear the shirt he'd claim off your back! Why, he's traded more cattle barons outta their fancy one-ups and sent them a-rattling off in some all-busted-up, old rimless buckboard pulled by a couple of matching sway-backs than you'd care to shake that short stick that he left you with at."

"Can you tell us where we might find him?" Cam felt the first swell of hope he'd experienced since they'd left St. Louis.

"Sure," the captain answered. "Just mention his name in Sedalia, and he'll find you. You'd be advised, though, to hold tight to the reins of these nice mounts of yours, or Ole Alcus'll leave you holding just your bridles."

It was at least 50 miles to Sedalia from the Boonville ferry, so they found a good camping spot that night next to a clear, rushing stream, where the horses had plenty to drink and eat. Dinner was quail eggs they'd rustled up, Cam handling the cooking duties this time.

"Would you please say Grace for us, Tad?"

"You go ahead and do it, Preacher. I ain't got the right words tonight."

Cam lowered his head and recited from memory, but his thoughts were on his companion. Tad had been especially quiet since leaving the ferry. When he dished up Tad's portion of the scrambled eggs and handed him the plate, he asked, "Aren't you excited? This is the closest we've gotten yet to locating you Pa."

"Sure, I's excited. It's just sorta scary, ya know…"

"I'm sure it must be." Cam turned to his own plate and decided to skip tonight's spelling lesson.

It wasn't hard to find. It took up an entire block of Sedalia's bustling business district, identified by a massive gilded sign with bright red lettering:

SMITH BROTHERS LIVERY
STABLE AND SALES
NEW AND USED WAGONS, BUCKBOARDS,
STAGECOACHES, HORSES

Before they could even dismount, they were greeted by a man who was almost as big around as he was tall. It looked as if the buttons were about to pop off of his vest, and his coat probably wouldn't button at all. Thinning black hair was combed forward onto his forehead, but what his head lacked was made up for by an abundant mustache that nearly covered his mouth.

"Alcus Smith's the name, trading's the game." He tapped a riding crop against his tall black boots as he approached Cam's mare and took hold of the bridle. "You ride 'em, we shoe 'em, you drive 'em, we sell 'em. Couple of nice mares you boys got there, but appears as though you been riding them right on into the ground. That cuts down on the price I can give you, but if you'd care to throw in the saddles and gear maybe we could..."

"We aren't here to sell our..." Cam tried to explain.

"Well then just take them on around back and the boys'll rub them down, feed them and shoe them for you." Smith waved his riding crop in the direction of the alleyway next to the corral.

"The fact is, we're not here for trading. We're looking for leads..."

"Leads? We got leads and bridles, saddle-horns and shoe-horns, saddlebags and some good ole nags. Come on in and let me show you some of our leathers. We got the finest leathers between here and..."

"No, listen." Cam raised his voice, a little desperate to make himself understood. "We really aren't interested in selling or buying. We're just after some information. We've been led to understand that you were with Canby through some campaigns down in Mississippi. "

"Yep, sure was." Smith circled Cam, running a discerning hand along the mare's rump, probably calculating what he could sell her for. "Wound up at the end of the war at a little place down there called Brookhaven. Thriving little community, it was, too. I even thought of opening myself up a little business down there and staying on after the war, you know, and just sending for my wife, Bernice. But I tell ya, I was just already so well established here with the family business in Sedalia that, well, I just decided to come on back. I been regretting it some, though, I gotta admit, not staying down there and all. I reckon I always will, sorta."

Smith fell momentarily silent, evidently lost in a memory, so Cam took the opportunity. "Yeah, well, that sounds good, but you see, we believe Tad's father joined up with one of the Negro units..." Campbell glanced back at the boy, still mounted on his own horse, listening intently.

"Well, that would've been with Bob Roy Floyd. Bob Roy spoke those black boys' language."

"Where can we find Floyd?" Cam quickly interjected before Smith could get going again.

"About ten miles south of here. Can't miss it. He has a big old chicken farm out there. Just ride south a piece and start listening for the roosters."

Cam touched his hat brim in a brief salute of thanks. "Much obliged, Mr. Smith. That is a great help."

As Cam tried to rein the mare around, Smith once again grabbed the bridle. "Sure I can't interest you in some fine new saddlebags? Looks like the ones you have there got a little scorched. We have a wide selection..."

"No, thank you very kindly, Mr. Smith," Cam smiled. "These'll do just fine." He gave the mare a gentle spur, she shook her head free of Smith's grip, and he and Tad headed back toward the dusty main street of Sedalia to head south.

But curiosity got the best of him. Cam reined around and returned a few paces back to inquire, "The sign says 'Smith Brothers'. Where's your brother?"

Stepping back onto center stage, grinning at the pleasure of having an audience again, Alcus took firm hold of the mount's bit, and comfortably continued. "Aw, there ain't no brother anymore... leastwise not in the business here. Bought him out years ago."

"I see," Cam managed to interject, gripping the reins tighter and pulling the horse free of Alcus' grasp one last time.

Undeterred, Smith prattled on. "Yeah, bother Lem and me was just young whipper-snappers when we started this here company out back in, well, lemme think now... it must've been back in the late thirties, I'd have to say... maybe a bit later...."

Smith's booming monologue mercifully became indistinguishable by the time Cam caught back up with Tad, who'd had the wisdom not to turn back. "I thought for sure I was gonna have to rescue you, Preacher, and just let ya ride double with me."

"Our salvation, m'lad, was that we never got off our steeds."

After a couple of hours of riding in silence, Cam was getting concerned. He tried for a third time to engage Tad in conversation. "Maybe we'll be able to buy a chicken from Mr. Floyd. That'd make for a real good dinner tonight, don't you think?"

When he got no response, he turned to look at Tad. The boy was staring down the road, lost in some other world. "Chicken for dinner tonight?" Cam prompted again.

Tad looked at him as if just remembering he wasn't alone. "Yeah, I reckon."

"Did your Ma have a special recipe for cooking chicken?"
"Fried."

Cam waited for more information, but none was forthcoming, so he left Tad to his brooding.

They'd only ridden another mile when they first heard the rooster that Alcus Smith had said would signal their approach to the Floyd farm. A substantial chicken barn took up most of the farm yard, looking like it was only one strong breeze away from collapsing under its own weight. Two roosters on opposite sides of the yard vied for domination, and hens scratched and pecked in the dust everywhere. On the far south side of the yard a modest white-washed house sat away from the barn at the edge of the woodland. A porch ran the length of the front, and two rocking chairs looked welcoming, but there was no one in sight.

"Hello! Anyone home?" Cam called as the horses ambled up to the porch rail.

Only the roosters answered.

A figure appeared briefly, pulling the window curtain back a crack, then disappeared. Moments later the front door opened, and a woman stood there in the doorway, her greying hair hanging in dirty strands around her thin face.

"Afternoon, ma'am." Campbell removed his hat and nodded. "I was wondering if this mightn't be..."

"Who's asking?" the woman spat.

"Excuse me, ma'am," Cam apologized. "My name's Campbell McCool, and this is my companion, Tad."

As Campbell dismounted, the woman stepped off the porch, wiping her hands on her apron. "Bob Roy's out to the barn yonder."

"Much obliged, ma'am."

"You ain't wanting to buy no liquor, are you?" she asked.

"No, ma'am. We're just passers-by," Cam assured her. He nodded his thanks again, but the woman had already turned and gone back into the house.

Cam led his horse toward the chicken barn, Tad following along, still mounted. "Hello... Mr. Floyd?"

"I hear'd ya!" The shout came from the dark interior of the barn. The man who appeared from the shadows was as gaunt and worn-looking as his wife, in overalls with ripped knees and muddy cuffs, and carrying a pitch fork.

"Mr. Floyd, my name's McCool, and I was hoping you might be able to help us out."

Floyd accepted Cam's handshake silently and cautiously.

With a brief glance up at Tad, Cam continued. "We were told that you were serving under Canby with Alcus Smith and the Sixty-Ninth Illinois Division, and that you led a Negro brigade down around Columbia, Mississippi."

"That's right." Floyd spit into the dust. "How can I help you?"

"Well, we've been trying for about a month now to locate my friend here's, father. We were thinking that he might've joined up with your boys there from Columbia."

Floyd reflected for a few moments, then scratched his head. "Old 'Stoker'?"

Campbell turned to look at Tad for some sign of recognition. There was none.

"Best damn blacksmith I ever seen," Floyd continued. "Could handle a bellows with his teeth whilst he shaped four shoes at oncest."

"That's him! That's my Pa! Best blacksmith Massah Ed ever had!" Tad exclaimed, practically bouncing in the saddle.

"'You'll find him over in Kansas City on the Kansas side of the river, last I recollect, working a stable there where the rivers meet. Still at it I reckon as far as I know, doing what he does best."

Cam exchanged a grin with Tad, then turned back to the chicken farmer. "We're much obliged, Mr. Floyd...much obliged indeed!" Cam thanked him as they shook hands again, then threw himself into the saddle. "Good day to you, Sir!" Cam saluted as he and Tad reined around and rode away, back down the dusty lane.

A LADY OF
THE THEATER

CHAPTER

8

THE ENTIRE COUNTRY must be heading west, Campbell thought as he and Tad maneuvered their horses around buggies and buckboards, horsemen and pedestrians crowding the dusty streets of Kansas City, Kansas, this warm evening. As they had crossed the river from Missouri into Kansas that afternoon, they'd passed a large gathering of conestoga wagons organizing into a train to follow either the Oregon Trail or the Santa Fe Trail toward new promise and opportunity. Although the sun was setting, shops were still open, and music and laughter spilled from the open doors of numerous saloons and dance halls. The town literally hummed with excitement and hope.

They'd stopped at a dry goods store to ask about Stoker Co, and the proprietor had given them exacting directions along side streets near the waterfront. The reverberating ringing of a blacksmith's hammer pinpointed the location before they saw the sign on the substantial barn-like building at the end of the street, next to the river.

Tad reined his horse to a halt in the middle of the street.

When Cam realized the boy had stopped, he pulled up and turned in his saddle. "Don't be nervous, Tad. He's your Pa."

"I knows that." Tad shifted uneasily. "Ya mind me and you meetin' up somewheres later?"

"Of course not. I understand. That's the way it should be. A son's reunion with his Pa's a private matter." Repressing a pang of disappointment, Cam reined his mare around to head back the way they'd come. "I tell you what. I'll go back to that hotel we passed and see if I can find some place to sleep other than in a bedroll for a change. You go on to your Pa, and I'll look you up tomorrow to say goodbye."

"Thanks, Preacher." Tad spurred his horse into a slow walk toward the sound of the pounding hammer.

"We'll say goodbye tomorrow," Cam called-out after him.

As Cam watched Tad cautiously approach the large barn doors, he wished he could be a fly on the wall to witness the joy on Tad's face as he reunited with the father he hadn't seen in more than a year. He'd tried to be a mentor and teacher to Tad during their weeks together, but a father's love was a precious and sacred thing and something only a true father could give. His disappointment swelled into a painful knot in his chest, and he kicked his mare into a trot back up the street.

The Palace Hotel didn't quite live up to its lofty name, but it was a substantial three-story building, recently painted red. In the rear, a livery stable was able to feed and bed down Annie. Now Cam would see what he might do to accommodate his own creature comforts.

The Palace Hotel sported a large porch with inviting rocking chairs, only one of which was occupied by a cowboy enjoying a cigar. The lobby and its furnishings were a little worn, but enticing aromas drifted from the dining room just visible through the arch to his left. A well-dressed clerk greeted him pleasantly from behind the long oak registration desk. "Good evening to you, sir."

"Good evening. A room for one, please."

"How long?" The desk clerk spun the register around for Campbell to sign, handing him a pen.

Cam scribbled his signature on the appropriate line. "Just overnight."

The clerk plopped a key down on the desk. "Three dollars."

"Three dollars!?"

"That's without a bath. Four dollars with." The clerk lifted his eyes in a lazy appraisal of Cam's road-weary appearance. "And it appears to me but what you might be needing four dollars worth."

Campbell shook his head, pulled the bills from his quickly shrinking stash, and slapped them down on the desk.

"Number 9. Top of the stairs, next to last room on your left. Bath's at the opposite far end of the hall."

"Of course it is," Campbell mumbled. "And I'll have that bath now, if it's not too much trouble." He grabbed the key and headed for the stairs.

After dropping his saddlebags in his room, Campbell went down the hall to avail himself of the bath privileges. Silently, the attendant, a Negro boy about Tad's age, carried in several buckets of steaming water, filled the tub, and placed a bar of lye soap and a clean towel on the nearby shelf. Cam had tried to ask him his name, but the boy just nodded subserviently, accepted a coin as tip, and scurried from the room. How totally different from the sprightly and chatty Tad, Cam mused.

After scrubbing himself well with the harsh soap, soaking in the tub until the one dollar's worth of hot water had turned so cold that he could hardly lie in it any longer, he climbed out, dried off, and returned, shivering, to his room. He found that the bath, while it had felt good, had left him no closer to being able to unwind. He had stayed in the cooling water too long, and it had rendered him more revived than relaxed.

He stretched out on the bed, the first real mattress he'd slept on in months, and stared at the ceiling. His thoughts were as fractured and scattered as the web of cracks in the plaster. Imagining the joyful reunion between Tad and his father brought a smile. And then it brought memories of his own father. The last time Cam had seen him was on that brief leave home in the fall of 1861. He'd looked gaunt and weary then, shouldering the burdens of war for all his parishioners, as well as the burdens of his own family. Cam would rather remember him as he'd been on the day he performed the ceremony that joined Cam and Mary Frances in holy matrimony—a strong, impassioned man of God, proud of his son and new daughter-in-law.

MAY 1 , 1861

Mary Frances picked up the screaming baby and held him to her shoulder, but little Davis wouldn't be comforted, and only screamed louder.

"Maybe he's hungry," Cam offered.

"I just fed him," she snapped. "He can't be hungry."

She was about to drop the child back into his cradle, but Cam reached out and gently took him from her, cradling the tiny creature in the crook of his arm. The baby hiccuped, and the wailing settled into a happy gurgle as he stared up at Cam.

Mary Frances collapsed into her rocker. "I still don't know why you have to go."

Campbell could hear the tears in her voice. Her lovely face seemed to be constantly swollen and red from crying lately, and there was nothing he'd been able to say or do to make it easier for her, to make her understand. He was past trying to be logical, and was having a hard time hiding his frustration. "We've been over this too many times to count. I can't think of any other way to explain it."

"Hundreds of other good doctors will be signing up. They don't need you. I need you. Your son needs you."

His son. They'd prayed long and hard for God to bless them with a child, and just as they'd received the news that the Yankees had attacked Fort Sumter, Mary Frances had given birth to this tiny, dark-haired miracle. Even now the thought still conjured in him a confusing muddle of emotions—pride, hope, fear, uncertainty, and downright awe. He'd never known he could love like this. Nor had he ever known such a rending dilemma. He needed to be here with his new family, and he needed to defend his home and honor his Hippocratic oath to ease suffering and save lives. It was an impossible decision that he prayed about constantly, as he watched Mary Frances grow more and more despondent and withdrawn.

Davis had settled back to sleep, so Campbell lay him gently in the cradle, then sat in the chair next to his wife, taking her hand in his. "I have a duty. An obligation. What kind of example would I be for our son if I neglected what I'm honor bound to do? I need to defend our home. For him."

She yanked her hand from his grip. "What about your obligation to me? I can't do this without you."

Cam sighed. This must've been the fifth time they'd had this conversation. "My parents are here. Mama is thrilled to have a grandchild to dote over. Or you could go back to your folks in Atlanta..."

And the conversation ended the same way all the others had. She burst into tears and rushed from the room.

Mary Frances. As he lay on the hard hotel mattress, her image returned to him as achingly vivid as it always did, as real and warm and yielding as she'd been on their wedding night. Pink, full lips that tasted of the wine they'd shared, and skin as smooth as satin, that tasted of salt and musk, and drove him to the edge of his self-control, blurring the line between lust and love. He knew she'd been with other men before him, but it had not mattered. Her skill at love-making made it all the more exciting, and he'd reveled in the pleasures they gave each other.

Neither was Campbell a novice at lovemaking, having had previous romantic entanglements always, at the given time, sensed to be *the* one.

He turned to his side, the familiar rising ache coming as no surprise. It had been a very long time since he'd held a woman and felt her warm, soft, supple flesh pressed against his bare skin. Perhaps because he had experienced the astounding beauty that could be shared by two lovers, true soul-mates, engaging in this blessed union, the option of settling for less now held little appeal for him.

His eyes came to focus on his saddlebags slung over the chair across the room. From the gilded leather portfolio tucked inside, the words lovingly copied onto good velum spoke to him. Although he knew them by heart, he needed to see and hold them. Cam rose and reached for the saddlebags, slipped the portfolio out from beneath his extra shirt, and settling back onto the bed, mouthed the words silently as he read.

ANNIVERSARY ODE

On a cold and wintry day
    Upon this Christmas Season -
A woman strolled into my life
    Without apparent reason -

But swiftly I was to recognize
    That face that person that being -
Since the absolute counterpart of my world
    Seemed to be within her seething.

Could she possibly be that special one-
    For whom my heart were reserved?
I could only learn that answer-
    If in me the senses she unnerved.

Yet how is one to be certain
    When fate deals such a hand -
Whether hers contains the finger-
    Upon which you're meant to place that band?

You encourage yourself toward incentive,
    As though you had some real choice -
And allow for possible introduction,
    While listening deeply within for a voice.

Such comes to you with little ado,
    And you gain still furthermore -
The knowledge in fact so crystal clear,
    That within her she bears your core.

Back to that period 'twas in 1860,
    And mind could n'er project -
That in so brief a span of time as this,
    Could be created so strong an effect.

The duration and beyond of this earthly tread,
    To share with one so new -
Was startling in the mere reckoning,
    For it happens so rarely and to few.

Yet all you found then to impose,
    This coupling met without strife -
'Til finally you accepted the obvious fate,
    That this woman was meant to become your wife.

She assumed the role and further still,
    She brought beyond all you knew -
An embellishment beyond even the dreams you held,
    Through her then you seemed to accrue.

She surely eventually did clearly reveal,
    That most intangible whole -
That innermost side of you that you'd fought,
    Which quite plainly had been your soul.

Not only did she bring that ultimate joy,
    Into your earthbound throng -
She demonstrated all to be so sound and true,
    That to each other you somehow belonged.

So now as time has led you here,
    Through experiences so vast -
Your prayer becomes in hopeful plea
    That, too, you've shared the past.

Tonight Campbell longed, as never before, for the pleasures of a woman. Not just for the physical release. He yearned with just as much ache for the true, deep, emotional connection that he'd believed he'd had with Mary Frances. When he'd last seen her, she'd changed into a person he did not recognize. She was unable to be the wife and mother he'd imagined her to be. But his woman must still be out there, the one God meant to be his soul's true companion. Their lives would come together. This, he had to believe.

Restless and uncomfortable, he rolled from the bed, pulled on his clothes, and headed downstairs to the restaurant, hoping that food would help assuage some of his need. He splurged on a large steak with all the trimmings and a bottle of wine, fully intending to drink all of it himself.

The restaurant was nearly full tonight, and as he ate he observed his fellow diners, and concocted stories that fit their appearances. The two well-dressed, middle-aged men in the center of the room were politicians, he decided, and over rare meat were debating the fate of their city. Three young cowboys stood at the bar, already uninhibited by having bathed their innards with alcohol. They were making ambitious plans for later in the evening. An elderly couple occupied the table near the door to the kitchen. They sat close together, but rarely spoke. He imagined they'd been together since childhood and no longer needed words to communicate, as their hearts and souls had merged into one, not unakin to the single-cell cosmos theory advance by Socrates... or was it Plato? Once he thought he'd had that. And one day he truly would, he reassured himself.

Almost as soon as he'd taken a seat, he'd noticed the woman sitting alone at a table at the end of the bar. She'd been watching the other patrons also, as she nibbled at her meal. Her elegant dress was a bright blue with silver trim, but modest, only giving hints of a nicely curved figure. Her golden hair was carefully styled and hung in ringlets to her shoulders. Once she had looked up and caught him staring at her. She'd graced him with an engaging little smile, but he'd quickly looked back down at his plate. He made up several stories for her, but he knew her real story was probably more intriguing than he could imagine.

The woman summoned the waiter, paid her bill, then rose from her table and sauntered slowly over toward Campbell. She was taller and more well endowed than he'd anticipated. "Good evening, Soldier," she greeted him softly.

Campbell's breath caught in his throat. But he was raised a good Southern gentleman. He rose and pulled a chair out for her, inviting her to join him, then returned to his own seat.

"You are a long way from home, aren't you?" Her voice sounded like an angel's and her delicate fragrance drifted across the table to him, that of some flower he couldn't quite identify.

When he failed to answer, she smiled and clarified, "I see from what's left of your uniform that you fought for Jeff Davis. Where do you call home?"

Campbell had hoped that the large meal, the wine, and the company of strangers would distract him from his uncomfortable desires, but he felt the involuntary flare of tension rise again, excited by her warmth and her scent.

He finally found his wits and his tongue. "Nowhere right now. Still looking for it, I guess. And you? I'm sure you don't call the Palace Hotel home." She exhibited class in abundance.

"The stage is my home." She laughed sweetly at her melodramatic delivery.

"Ah... a 'lady of the theater'. Well, that is an instinctive need in all of us at that, isn't it?"

"What need do you mean?" The lady touched the empty glass sitting in front of her.

Campbell picked up the bottle and filled the glass. "To communicate... to be understood."

"I don't know that I take myself as seriously as all that. I'm just an entertainer, an ex-lady-of-the-chorus-line who learned to like the warmth of the footlights, down stage." She lifted her glass in a toast, and Cam joined her. As they each sipped the dark, sweet liquid, her blue eyes never left his.

"And about you and your soldiering?" She set her glass on the table and ran a delicate, red-lacquered fingernail around the rim.

Cam studied his own glass. "I've learned not to like the coldness of soldiering."

The lady reached over and placed a warm hand on Campbell's, leaving it there, and her smile faded. "You've been hurt, Soldier."

"No...no, I'm fine," he quickly insisted.

"I don't mean just by the war. It's all over your face."

"Everybody's had those kinds of hurts. Sorta goes with the territory."

"'Love's Labors Lost', I suppose." She took Cam's hand in both of hers now, squeezing firmly, her heat coursing through him like warm honey. This lady must be magnificent on the stage, he decided.

He corralled his racing thoughts and turned the subject back to her. "And where might one be privileged to see you performing on this stage of yours?"

The lady pulled her hands back from Campbell's and fondled the stem of her wine glass with her lovely, slender fingers. "She's appearing every evening until further notice at the Theater Royal as Leila, a singing bayadere, in Auber's popular ballet-opera, 'The Maid of Cashmere'," she announced as though reading from a playbill.

"And who is she, this lady 'appearing'?"

"She, Soldier, is Miss Rebecca Messent." She lifted her glass for another sip, looking over its rim and directly into the center of his desire.

"And is she?" Cam smiled.

"Is she what?"

"A 'maid'?"

Miss Messent coyly returned the smile. "Certainly no maiden can she claim to be in the Biblical sense." She paused, taking another sip of wine, making it a much more sensual gesture than it needed to be. "And you?"

"You what?" Cam blinked.

"More than a soldier?"

"Feeling, at this moment, far more 'soldier' than 'reverend'."

"Ah, a man of the cloth?"

Was that disappointment he saw in her eyes? "And of the flesh. . . in the Biblical sense," Cam amended.

A long-forgotten quote filtered into Campbell's muddled thoughts. 'Who knows the longings of the human heart and the soul's vast yearnings? Frustration breeds strange children of the night and. . . dark mourning'. Although he couldn't recall its author, he now realized its real meaning. He sensed that tender would be this night, and dark, then, tomorrow morning.

STOKER CO
HELLFIRE'S BRIMSTONE

CHAPTER

9

It sounded like home—the ringing of the massive hammer hitting the anvil. Tad remembered how he could just barely lift that hammer, and he'd always marveled at how his Pa could swing it like it was a willow switch. He sat quietly as his horse swished her tail and shifted anxiously, like she could tell what he was feeling or should do next. This was the moment he'd been thinking on and dreaming about forever. And now he was here, and it wasn't a dream anymore. It felt real and heavy, like the shiny, forbidden thing he'd been hiding in his bedroll since leaving the riverboat, that now was a daunting weight in his pocket. He took a deep breath, slid from the saddle, and headed toward the open stable door.

Inside the smokey, airless stable, Jerod "Stoker" Co had his back to the door, concentrating on the horseshoe he was pounding. His powerful black arms, dripping with sweat, glistened in the red glow of the burning coals. When he paused in his hammering to examine his work, he must've sensed he was no longer alone, and turned to face his intruder.

"Tad?" The big man blinked and swiped the sweat from his eyes. "That you, boy?"

Tad could barely force the words out of his throat. "Yeah, Pa."

"Why, good ol' Tademus!" Stoker dropped the hammer and started towards him. "I never expected to see you again. How'd you get yourself all the way up in these parts, boy?"

Tad took a step back, and from his pocket pulled out the small pistol. "Don't come no closer."

Stoker stopped in his tracks. "Now, you just hold on, boy. You just wait one second. What's this you fixin' to do? You can't be a holding no bad blood betwixt us after all this time."

Tad felt those cold, black eyes lock onto him, and the old familiar terror churned in his stomach again.

"Now you just listen up to your ol' man for just one damn minute." Stoker's hands tightened into huge, hard fists, as solid as the hammer, and he took another threatening step forward. "It was the war. The war done real bad things, boy. But that there's all behind us now. We just gotta forgit and go on..."

"No war kilt my Ma," Tad spat. "And it's gonna take a heap longer than no year 'fore I forgets how she DO die."

"Son, your ol' Pa was just all likkered up! You was there. You saw. It was a accident. You can't go on a blamin' me about your Ma."

It for sure hadn't been the first time his Pa had come back to the cabin full of moonshine and meanness, angry at anything he could lay his big hands on. Tad's Ma had always been able to protect him, but that dark, cold night had been different, and it had never left Tad's head. It had become the ghost that haunted his sleep, the reason he got up every day, and the reason the devil had made him steal the vest pistol from the gentleman-gambler's cabin on the Nachez Belle. And now he could finally get that devil off his back for good. His finger tightened on the trigger.

Stoker barked out that horse-like laugh of his. "Besides, what harm you figuring you gonna do with that little ol' pop-gun?"

Tad glanced around at the smokey, fiery blacksmith's pit, as close to hell as he'd ever imagined, and he had the sudden need to run as far away as he could get. This had all been different in his dreams, a whole lot easier. He'd never killed anyone, not for real, and he knew he couldn't do it now. He came to a sudden decision, pushing the devil behind him, and lowered the gun. "I been thinking on it long and hard how I'd see you dead. But you already in hell anyways, and that sure where you bound to go when you DO dies."

With a sudden, powerful lunge, Stoker grabbed Tad by the front of his shirt and walloped him hard across the face. Tad flew backward, skidding across the floor.

Through blurred vision, he watched his Pa's thick bulk amble toward him, eyes shining fierce, glowing almost as red as the light from the fire. Stoker raised his fist to strike again. "Looks like you done lost all respect for your ol' Pa. I's just gonna hafta beat it back into you then. . ."

Tad scooted backward, trying to get out of reach of those long arms, and heard himself begging like he was a small child again, "No, Pa, please don't. . . please."

Stoker swung a sweeping fist down across Tad's head with the stunning blow rolling him across the floor like a log, slamming him against a large, block table.

Stoker raged toward him again.

Cornered and panicked, his head ringing like a struck anvil, Tad desperately grasped upward, scrabbling for some kind of purchase to pull himself up. His hand closed around cold iron, something solid and heavy. He grasped it and swung with all his strength.

The metal tongs smashed into the side of Stoker's head with a sickening thud. Blood spurted into Tad's face. Stoker's eyes rolled back in his head and he collapsed into a lifeless heap next to Tad's own body.

Then everything went dark.

DARK MOURNING
BECOMES
A DARK MORNING

CHAPTER

～ 10 ～

Brand new and gleaming white, the Alabama State Hospital for the Insane looked more like a fancy hotel than a medical facility, Cam had thought as he'd guided the carriage through the high stone obelisks that flanked the entrance of the long gravel drive. He'd read the literature and talked with colleagues, and he knew in his heart that this was the best place for Mary Frances and little Davis. Still, leaving them here among strangers, no matter how knowledgeable, dedicated and compassionate, felt to Cam as if he were locking them away in a prison.

On the carriage ride out from town, Davis had lain in a basket on the seat between them. When he wasn't sleeping, he was gurgling and babbling happily in his own little six-month-old language, enthralled by the world passing by, totally innocent of the forces that were tearing that world apart around him. Mary Frances, pressed far to the opposite side of the seat, never noticed. Never spoke to the child, never touched him. Silent and still, she had stared into the distance, lost in some realm he couldn't touch or see. Cam did not know this woman she'd turned into. She had become a woman who looked upon her own husband as though he were a stranger. They'd not taken that lifetime to say "I knew thee well". She'd become a woman repulsed by any human contact with her own son... unable to hold him or even to touch him.

At first Cam had attributed Mary Frances' uncontrollable crying, sudden angry outbursts, and mounting frustration at caring for Davis, to his decision to enlist in the Confederate Army. He was wrenched in half, much as his country was, needing to heed the call of honor and duty while his country faced its darkest days, but also needing to support Mary Frances, the other half of his soul, in her transition into motherhood. Knowing that she and the baby were in the loving embrace of his family in Mossy Point, he'd made his final decision, and he could only hope and pray that he was being receptive to the will of his Heavenly Father.

His mother had told him that sometimes, after giving birth, new mothers will feel afraid and sad, inadequate at taking care of their child. It was a natural state. But as soon as they got to know the baby and found a routine, they'd snap out of it. Mary Frances hadn't. For months, the letters from home became increasingly disturbing. He could read the fear and anxiety between the lines of his mother's long missives. Mary Frances wrote of mundane things—the weather, the chickens, the garden. In her last letter she'd simply apologized for not being the wife and mother he wanted her to be, while remaining lucid enough to express her incompatibility with these roles. Then she stopped writing altogether.

A colleague at the Confederate Army Hospital where he worked had recommended Dr. Peter Bryce and the Alabama State Hospital for the Insane.

Insane. It was not a word he would ever want to associate with the sweet, sparkling, dark-haired girl who had come into his life and filled a void he hadn't known existed. He felt as if their souls meshed like two long-missing pieces of a larger puzzle—again, imaging from the Dialogs of Plato. Now he stood helplessly and watched her disappear down the seemingly *endless hospital hallway between two white-clad nurses, one of them carrying their child. She had not even spared him a backward glance. He felt the painful cracks of that void gaping open again.*

A hand rested lightly on his shoulder, and the calming voice intruded on his thoughts. "This kind of thing is not unheard of, and we've developed some new, promising treatments."

Cam blinked back to reality. "Yes, I've been reading. . . " He turned to face Dr. Bryce, a man not much older than himself. The neatly trimmed beard and broad mustache gave Bryce's open, honest smile a mature, professional demeanor.

"Rest assured, Dr. McCool, your wife and son will receive the very best of care, and I will send weekly updates on her progress. Why don't I show you around?"

Dismissing the gut-wrenching feeling that he'd never see his wife and son again, Cam managed a smile. "Thank you, Doctor. I'd like that."

Campbell woke abruptly, the frighteningly haunting remnants of the vague nightmare clinging to the edges of his mind. Then he saw the divinely exquisite feminine form of Rebecca Messent lying next to him, still asleep, and he remembered the ecstasy of their night-long love-making.

This wasn't the 'dark mourning' he had imagined he would be facing. There wasn't the surging remorse he'd expected for having shared his bed, among other things, with this beautiful, warm stranger. He reached up to push a wayward lock of silky golden hair from her forehead, and watched her ample breasts swell gracefully with each breath, just as his desire for her began to swell again within him. Between their passionate, physical intimacy, they had also shared an intellectual familiarity, talking quietly of books and plays and music, until the overwhelming carnal needs took hold again. Was this a lingering lust, or did his soul recognize her? Could he perhaps grow to love her? How would he know?

Whether it were love or lust he was feeling, there was another important matter impelling him to get out of bed. Campbell dressed quietly and went downstairs to await some word from Tad. He walked over to the bar in the dining room and ordered coffee from the bartender.

When the bartender set the cup in front of him and started pouring the thick, steaming liquid, Cam asked him if he knew where the Negro blacksmith Stoker Co lived.

The bartender startled, letting the coffee overflow the cup. "Haven't you heard? A man named Co was killed last night."

Panic gripped Cam around the throat. "A little Co? I mean a little boy named Co?"

"No, a Negro blacksmith, like you were asking..."

"Where is he... the little boy, I mean?"

"They're holding a boy over to the jail, that they say done it."

But Campbell was already halfway out the door.

By the time Cam reached the Sheriff's office a couple of blocks away, he'd regained some of his composure. When he slammed through the front door, the jailer behind the desk looked up from his reading. "You'd be McCool, I make it."

"Where's the boy?"

Putting down his magazine, the jailer pushed himself back from the desk, rose lazily from the chair, and headed toward a door at the rear of the office, grabbing a ring of keys from a peg on the wall on the way.

Campbell followed closely on his heels as they entered the cell block. There were four cells, two on either side of the passageway. The jailer led Campbell to the first cell on the right, where Tad sat huddled up in a corner, away from the cell's other occupant, a drunken bum who reeked of cheap liquor.

"What's the boy doing in there with him?"

"Listen, Mister McCool, it just gives me one less cell to scald out. I got me more to do than to go around cleaning up after drunks and killers."

Campbell glared at the jailer, his temper beginning to rise like boiling water. "Get the boy outta there," he hissed.

The jailer turned and unlocked the cell. "Alright, hold your horses. C'mon, little nigger, you come on outta there."

Campbell grabbed the jailer violently by the shirt, spun him around, and slammed him hard back against the bars, moving in nose to nose. "The boy's name is Tademus."

The jailer's eyes bulged.

"Call him by his name," Cam demanded.

The jailer stammered wordlessly. Again Cam slammed him against the cell bars. "Say it!"

"Tademus," the terrified jailer sputtered.

Campbell released his grip, giving the man an extra shove. "Now open another cell."

Tad pushed to his feet, keeping as far from the jailer as he could get, and when the jailer opened the cell across the passageway, Tad trod over and headed into the far corner to slump back to the floor.

Campbell followed him in, then turned to face the jailer as the door slammed shut. The jailer, now separated from Campbell by the bars, got his tongue and his courage back. "If it don't matter none to the white one, then why'd it make no never mind to the black one?"

Campbell glared at him through the bars. The idiot didn't seem to know when to let well enough alone.

"So what's that little darkie to you anyways?" the jailer challenged.

Campbell's temper boiled over again. Reaching through the bars, he grabbed the man by the shirtfront and jerked him forward, crushing his face hard against the iron. "You're working right out there on the edge, turn-key. When I say, you're gonna have to come back in here and open up this door for me. I'd be thinking real hard on that if I were you."

The jailer pulled his shirt from Cam's grip and quickly exited the way they'd entered.

After the door had closed, Campbell turned to Tad, still huddled in the corner. "You all right, Tademus?" He felt in this gut-wrenching moment an overwhelming concern for his little charge, along with total helplessness like he'd never before experienced in his lifetime. Again, as when he'd left his infant son, he could only rely on the wisdom of the Almighty to guide him now.

Cam stood for a few moments in silence gazing at Tad, who sat on the floor with his head bowed and an expression of ineffable fear and anxiety on his tear-streaked face. Finally Cam squatted down on the floor, assuming a seated position next to his little pal.

"What's gonna become of me now, Camel? They gonna just get shut of me?"

For the first time ever, even though mispronounced, Tad had addressed his 'Preacherman' by his proper given name. Campbell put his arm around Tad's skinny shoulders and pulled him into a close embrace. "Not so long as I've got breath, Tademus."

MY WOMAN'S CARESS

CHAPTER

11

TAD HAD LOST EVERY GAME of checkers they had played that afternoon, even the ones Campbell had tried to let him win. Cam was nervous, too, about the final court hearing tomorrow morning, and leaving Tad alone in the jail cell that evening had felt like a betrayal of everything he'd ever told the lad.

Over the past couple of weeks, Cam had tried to create some stability and routine in Tad's life, to counteract the effects of having to live in a cold, hard cell, with his only company being the occasional drunk or rabble-rouser in the next cell. Cam had been there every morning when Tad's breakfast was delivered, and he'd often bring treats—some hard candy or a piece of pie from the hotel kitchen. They spent the mornings with the slate and chalk, and the McGuffey's Reader Cam had convinced the local school teacher to loan him. After lunch, they played checkers or dominoes, and he started to teach Tad chess. Sometimes they'd talk, or tell stories. Sometimes they'd just sit together in the warm silence. At dinner time, Cam would choose a favorite Bible passage to read before saying grace.

But the Sheriff closed-up promptly after the evening meal was brought in so Cam had left the boy sitting alone on his cot that evening, frowning down at his fried chicken and string beans. The cell block door had clanged closed behind Cam with a solid finality.

Back at the Palace Hotel, Cam had only been able to take a couple bites of his own chicken before giving up and taking his beer back up to Rebecca's room. He would be eternally grateful to her for offering to share her accommodations. Paying for a room for days on end while Tad's case crept its way through the court system was not within his current budget, so he'd planned to camp out near the river at the edge of town. Sharing a soft feather bed with the enticing and generous Miss Messent was much more comfortable in so many ways.

As he awaited Rebecca's return from her nightly performance, he sat in the brocade chair by the window, his glass of beer on the table next to him, his Bible open in his lap. But even God's word couldn't distract him from what was to take place tomorrow—the final hearing that would decide Tad's fate.

Several hearings had already been held. The judge had heard witnesses and reviewed evidence. He'd asked pertinent questions and listened carefully to the answers. He seemed to be a fair man. Surely in this new era of freedom and justice for the Negro race, he'd not hold Tad to a different standard than he would any other child who was trying to defend himself against an abuser. But Cam just didn't know. He had been learning the hard way that love, harmony, and forgiveness could not be legislated. No matter what the laws of man decreed, hatred, bitterness and revenge would continue to fester in the hearts of man, until the day he returned to the higher laws of God. Teaching and preaching the Word would not be enough. The only way Cam could think of truly to foster that kind of transformation was by example. He had come to believe that God had gifted him with Tad's companionship, and the love and commitment that had grown to accompany it, as an earthly demonstration of the meaning of the verse from Matthew—"Suffer little children, and forbid them not, to come unto me: for of such is the kingdom of heaven." It was not going to be an easy thing, this task God had assigned him.

He hadn't realized he'd dozed off until Rebecca lifted the drooping Bible from his hands and kissed him lightly on the forehead. "You'd be much more comfortable in bed, Soldier."

She'd already changed into her long, red silk robe, and washed off the thick stage makeup. The fragrance of lavender soap filled his head, and he swam in her deep blue eyes. He rose to slip his hands beneath the robe and slid it from her shoulders, then pulled her into a deep kiss he was just realizing he needed badly.

She usually returned from her nightly performances exhausted. He thought she'd fallen asleep, curled up next to him. But as sated as their love-making had left him, sleep still evaded him. He carefully scooted from beneath her arm and sat up against the headboard, lighting the candle on the bedside table. Gently he lifted the portfolio of poetry, and in the dim bubble of light from the candle, flipped through the pages. These words that had come from his heart so long ago, in that other lifetime, had transformed from painful reminders into comforting mementos of happier times. At the bottom of the slim stack, he found...

MY WOMAN'S CARESS

A tropical flower floats down meandering stream -
Only too few know that fulfilled dream.
We left love to rest with senses oh so keen -
That those precious memories are still the loveliest seen -

That tender warmth of my woman's caress.

While seizing yesterday's dream may enrich today,
Let us never encourage a new love's delay.
In passion's sweet lust we knew but one soul -
That neither time nor distance could ever turn cold -

That tender warmth of my woman's caress.

Her face may change but she'll ever be to me -
The vision of gentle beauty that only I can see.
Regretting never the dissolve of a love as such -
Still tonight with someone else I felt her touch -

That tender warmth of my woman's caress.

We found the key to unlock all treasures -
And tasted the nectar of life's pure pleasures.
Enriched by all the senses of the flesh,
Our two souls became as one between us meshed.

That tender warmth of my woman's caress.

Our hearts were aflame with love that was right -
For neither time nor distance can filter out the light.
The embers shall smolder 'til time is no more,
And perhaps even then we'll share as before -

That tender warmth of my woman's caress.

The love that for this earthly life's been told -
In memory so real can never grow cold.
Sustained by assurance we've lived life His way -
We know we'll in Heaven be reunited some day.

That tender warmth of my woman's caress.

"You are distracted tonight, aren't you?" Her quiet words brought him back to the present.

"It's that obvious, is it?" He returned the slip of paper to the folder, placed it back on the table, and blew out the candle.

She pushed up next to him and leaned companionably against him, shoulder to warm shoulder. "You're worried about tomorrow."

"You do read me like a book, Miss Messent."

Taking his hand and slipping her long fingers between his, she squeezed gently. "You wear your heart on your sleeve when it comes to that little boy."

"I know. I'm sorry. But it should be no concern of yours. Go back to sleep."

"Don't be silly. Of course it's my concern. What hurts you, hurts me."

Cam drew in a deep breath. He hadn't meant for this to happen, but it had somehow gotten out of his control. He pulled his fingers from hers and put his arm around her shoulders, pulling her tight against him. "I'm not sure what I did to deserve you, Miss Beck, but whatever it was, it must've been mighty powerful."

The silence hung between them in the velvet darkness, the only sound the call of a night bird in the distance through the open window, the only sensation her heart beating close to his. Whatever happened tomorrow, he knew it would inevitably change this, what he'd come to yearn for every night, what had eased his ache, revived his spirit, and lightened his heart.

"You've not told Tademus about us, have you?"

"No, I haven't." It had been an unconscious decision, something he'd felt in his gut. Now he searched for words to explain it. "I'm all he has in this world. He doesn't need anything else weighing on his mind right now."

"Surely the judge will see the truth and consider his age. Everything will work out."

"I wish I knew that for a certainty."

She sat up straight, pulling away from him, leaving a chill where there had been warmth. "Campbell, these past few weeks have been wonderful. And you must know that if there were to be an 'us', that it would certainly include Tad, no matter what the court decides."

He turned to look at her, wishing he could see her face more clearly. "That is a noble and generous offer, but..."

She silenced him with a finger against his lips. "But you have something else you need to do if your heart is ever truly to be free, and that will take you away from here."

Whatever he'd done to deserve her must've been exceptionally extraordinary. His mouth found hers, her arms encircled his neck, and they slid back beneath the sheets to revel in the pleasure of each other one more time. When she finally drifted off into a peaceful sleep, he lay listening to her breathe, and stared at the ceiling.

MY SON...MY BROTHER

CHAPTER
~ 12 ~

WHEN CAM ENTERED through the rear doors of the cavernous, high-ceilinged courtroom, the judge was already on the bench, sorting through paperwork with his bailiff. Fancy gold letters on the little plaque in front of him read "Judge Thomas M. Logan". Several other people were scattered around on the hard wooden pews that made up the complement, evidently awaiting their own appointment with justice. Tad was seated at the defendant's table between the Sheriff and his annoying deputy. Between the two burly men, Tad looked like a fragile rag doll. That image can only help our cause, Cam thought as he pulled another chair up to the table and pushed himself between Tad and the deputy. Tad had huddled back into his chair, his arms hugged tightly around himself, but his eyes brightened when Cam sat next to him. Cam hoped his own smile showed confidence and faith instead of the dread that actually knotted his stomach. He kept his tone light. "Did you have a good breakfast?"

"It was good. Didn't have no meat, though."

Cam had to grin at Tad's attempt at humor. It was a good sign.

The room grew silent at the sound of the judge's gavel. "We have before us the case of the State of Kansas versus one Tademus Co. Are all parties present?"

The Sheriff stood, his hat in his hands. "We are, Your Honor."

"Very good." Judge Logan scratched his signature on the piece of paper in front of him. "It is the judgment and rendering of this circuit court that the actions of one Tademus Co against his father, Jerod 'Stoker' Co, were exercised in self-defense."

Tad looked up at Cam, his eyebrows knitted in confusion. Cam gave him an encouraging pat on the shoulder as the judge continued. "The boy is hereby remanded into the custody of the local authorities and is to be interned on the county farm at Whitfield until such time as he reaches his twenty-first birthday."

Visions of hard labor in the blazing sun and barracks crowded with older ruffians swarmed into Cam's head. Next to him, Tad sniffled and pulled his knees up in front of him, clasping them to his chest.

Cam stood, "If I may, your Honor..."

"Mr. McCool...?" Judge Logan lowered his head and studied Cam over his spectacles as Cam approached.

"Well, Sir," Cam began, "Tad and I have been traveling companions for quite some time now."

"State your case, Mr. McCool," the Judge hastened, turning back to his paper work.

"If it pleases the court, your Honor, I would like very much to assume custody of Tademus." Behind him he heard Tad's small gasp and the murmurings of the spectators.

"This presents a most unusual consideration, you doubtlessly are aware, Mr. McCool." Logan studied him again critically. "Under such an arrangement, you would, in fact, be required to adopt, legally, this lad."

"I do understand fully, your Honor, and I would accept that responsibility."

Logan stared a hole through him. For a brief second, Cam was sure the judge was going to laugh out loud and deny his request. "Well, off the record and in all candor, I cannot say as how I readily recognize the practicality of so unlikely an arrangement." He removed his spectacles and cleaned them with the long, loose sleeve of his black robe. "However, if this is your desire and your decision, be it so ruled. Sheriff, you'll see to the necessary documents and have the procedure properly notarized."

The Sheriff shot to his feet. "Yessir, your Honor."

"This hearing stands adjourned." The bang of the gavel announced the end of the session.

Campbell turned and was nearly knocked over when Tad slammed into him, throwing his bony arms around Cam's waist in a tight hug, tears choking his voice. "I love you, Preacherman."

Campbell returned the hug, feeling like he might crush the boy if he squeezed too tightly. "I love you, too, Tademus Co of Marion County, Mis'sippi."

LOVES' LABOURS LOST

CHAPTER

13

OVER TAD'S HEAD, Cam saw Rebecca rise from the last pew. Their eyes locked and she gave him a wan smile before turning quietly to leave the courtroom.

Although they'd had to wait a while for the Sheriff to put together the appropriate papers, it hadn't taken long to sign everything and have it all properly notarized. Tad had insisted on holding the piece of paper that declared him to be the legal ward of Davis Campbell McCool, but when they got back to the Palace Hotel for Cam to gather his things, Campbell made sure to tuck it safely inside his jacket pocket before they retrieved the horses and headed out of town.

As they approached the brightly painted Theater Royal, Cam reined his mare over to the sidewalk. "I need to take care of something before we leave," he told Tad as he dismounted.

She must've seen them ride up. She came out before Cam had reached the big brass-trimmed double doors, and she laid a gloved hand on his arm.

"I saw you in the courtroom," Cam stated simply.

Rebecca nodded. "You're doing the right thing, Soldier."

"So..." Cam drew in a long breath and squinted up at the bright sky, struggling to keep his tone light. "You're sure that we haven't met somewhere before?"

A brief little smile lifted the corners of her pretty lips. "That's supposed to be an opening line, Soldier, not a closing one."

"Ah ha! That's where I've been going astray."

There was a long moment of silence as Campbell lost himself for the last time in her blue eyes. "I do believe I recognize you, Miss Rebecca Messent. And I know that I'm going to miss you... I'm going to miss you very much."

"Believe me, Solider... there's nothing about Miss Messent that you missed."

Indeed, he had not. But he certainly would for many nights to come and likely beyond.

He couldn't bare to see the tears welling in her eyes, so he drew her close, and she returned his embraced. Softly, he whispered into her ear, "Rebecca, please don't... "

Carefully, she pushed away from him, stepped back, and with her head held high, she smiled up at him. "Good-bye, Campbell. Good luck to you and the boy."

Cam climbed into the saddle before he could change his mind, and reined his horse around to join Tad, watching from the street. He didn't look back as they trotted east, out of Kansas City.

They were well out of town before Tad finally broke the silence. "You ever had a woman all your very own, Preacherman? I mean like you was all her'n and she was all your'n?"

Cam had visited that very consideration for so long he'd almost learned to live with it and certainly had no words now to answer Tad, so he offered none. The silence was deafening.

But Tad couldn't let that silence hang between them for long. "Don't you reckon as how it's about time you answered that there question I asked you way back in Mis'sippi?"

"What question might that be, my inquisitive young sir?"

"Where's you headin', Preacherman?" Then Tad quickly corrected himself. "I mean to say, that is, where WE headin'?"

"Well, Tademus, I was figuring we might ride on down Jefferson City way."

"Jefferson City? You reckon maybe some folks down there needs preaching to and saving, do you?"

A pang of apprehension tightened in Cam's chest, and the little tintype suddenly felt heavy in his shirt pocket. But he wasn't about to let anything weight too heavily on this beautiful early summer day. "Well, the Gospel can work its miracle most anyplace, I suppose. But there's also a family down that way I'd like to get to know."

"This family, they friends of your'n ?"

"Nope, can't claim so yet."

Again, Tad puzzled on this for a brief moment. "If'n these here folks ain't friends of your'n, then how come we ridin' all the way down to Jefferson City to look 'em up?"

"Well, I can't see any harm in our cultivating their friendship, can you?"

"Cultivate, you say! You ain't tellin' me we 'bout to give up preachin' now and set in to farmin', are you?"

Cam grinned at Tad's teasing and at the glorious, sunny day. "Not a chance. Not yet, anyway." One of the spirituals Tad had taught him had been buzzing in his ear, and now it bubbled up inside him with such force that he had to let it escape. "This little light of mine, I'm going to let it shine. Oh, this little light of mine, I'm going to let it shine...."

Tad laughed out loud, the sweetest sound he'd heard in weeks, and joined right in with his boyish tenor. "Hallelujah, this little light of mine, I'm going to let it shine. Let it shine, let it shine, let it shine!" And they were in harmony.

THE WAR AIN'T OVER

CHAPTER

14

T AD'S MOUTH WAS WATERING for some fatback this morning, or even a piece of fried rabbit. But they'd finished off all their meat two days ago and hadn't been able to catch anything since. Fish just wasn't the same as good ol' red meat. But Tad looked up from stirring the mush to watch the Preacherman as he finished his bathing in the river. He'd give up meat any day for sharing mush with that man.

He hadn't known many white men in his life. There'd been Massah Ed and his son, Young Massah. And the overseer, Ezekiel. Compared to other plantation owners he'd heard tell of, those three weren't so bad. But Campbell was different. With Campbell, he felt safe and cared for, even loved. He'd heard his elders talk about freedom, and the joys they'd imagined it would bring, but it always seemed to Tad like something out of a fantasy story. Somewhere along this journey, though, he'd stopped fearing being back-handed for speaking out, or whipped for making a mistake. This must be what 'free' really felt like.

Campbell sang to the treetops as he splashed in the water. He had a nice enough voice, but he sure couldn't get the tune right. Cam took a break from scaring the birds to ask, "Tademus, m'lad, aren't you finished with our breakfast, yet?"

Tad gave the mush another good stir, scraping up what was sticking to the bottom of the pot. "First, I gets the wood, then I builds the fire, then I boils the coffee, then I cooks the mush, and stirs it, and stirs it..."

"Tad, I say..." Cam called out, again.

"I hears ya, I hears ya!! If you'd get yourself outta that there creek and lend a hand, we'd been already done eatin' by now!"

"Cleanliness is next to Godliness, you know." Cam climbed from the river as naked as a newborn, dripping water. He grabbed the old flour sack they used as a towel and began scrubbing himself dry. "Next town we come to, we gotta get us some proper towels. This croakersack's killing."

"Whatsamatter? It scratch your tender skin, do it?"

"My, my. Did we get outta the bedroll on the wrong side this morning?"

"I can tell you one thing sure. Some of us got outta our'n way 'fore others of us even open no eye!"

Campbell leaned over the pot, checking Tad's progress. "So how's it coming along anyway?"

"Without no meat's how it comin' along, that's how." Tad complained, trying to hide his smile. "Fact is, I just about done even forgot how a slab of fatback smells a fryin' up in a hot skillet. And I know I done forgot how it taste! I's gonna wither up and die if'n I don't start eatin' right."

"Well, we'll be restocking before nightfall, I'd say." Cam draped the wet flour sack over a branch and pulled on his long johns, buttoning them up. "I calculate Jeff City's not more than twenty, maybe thirty miles on."

"Then it be your week for cooking chores," Tad reminded.

"Well, that's right, Tad. Of course, we're gonna be in town doing us some fine cafe-eating during *my* week of cooking."

"Aw, c'mon now, Camel. That ain't gonna count!" Tad wanted to pretend he was offended at Cam's teasing, but he just couldn't. He'd take care of this man's horse, cook all his meals, and give him the moon if he asked for it. So Tad grinned down into the bubbling mush and said a quick prayer of thanks to that God the Preacherman was always going on about.

Meanwhile, the Preacherman picked up with his cater-wauling, this time with a new hymn. "Wash all my sins a-way, dear Lord. . .wash all my sins ah-a-way. Must Jees-sus face the cross ah-lone. . . ."

The crack of a dry branch startled them both. Tad turned to look at the two horsemen just emerging from the tree line. They wore faded, frayed Union blue, and the older one carried a sturdy, shiny rifle across his saddle. The younger one, the blonde one, addressed his partner. "My, but don't he sing purdy, Howard?"

"Might nigh like an angel, I'd have to say." Howard flashed a gap-toothed grin.

Campbell pulled on his equally faded and frayed Confederate uniform pants and circled Tad to stand between him and the newcomers. "I apologize if I disturbed your morning, gentlemen. Will you join us in breaking our fast?"

"What you doing here, Reb?"

"Washing myself in this lovely river and praising with song, as you heard."

"What you're doing is trespassing," Howard spat. "This here's Barker land you're on."

Slowly, carefully, Campbell picked up a tin plate from the log by the fire and scooped some of the hot mush from the pot. Tad took the plate when Cam handed it to him, then Cam reached for another and ladled out more mush. "Well, I offer my apologies to Mister Barker. I didn't know this was posted land." Cam extended the second plate of mush to Howard. "Offer you boys some breakfast in return?"

With a swift swing, Blondie dashed the plate from Cam's hand, splattering hot mush in all directions. "This ain't just no ordinary trespasser, Howard. What we got us here is a Rebel infiltrator."

Cam shifted and tensed, his hands balling into fists. "Like I said, I'm sorry if we've transgressed. I'll happily offer your Mister Barker something for the night's lodging and hospitality."

"It's Colonel," Howard corrected. "Colonel Barker. And he don't run no hotel, Reb."

Swinging the business end of his shiny rifle around and pointing it at Cam's chest, Howard ordered, "Mount on up, Soldier-boy, and your little darkie slave boy, there, too."

Tad jumped up and pushed past Cam. "I ain't no slave..."

Cam's sudden tight grip on his shoulder shut him up. Cam's voice was just as tight. "Let's go pay a visit to Colonel Barker, Tad. I'm sure we can work out this little misunderstanding."

"But Camel..."

Cam's grip clamped harder. "Douse the fire while I saddle the horses."

All during the ride from their camp site, Campbell had stayed close to Tad, keeping him at his side, while Blondie led the way and Howard followed, rifle still at the ready. The house they finally approached was smaller than Massah Ed's big house, but this Colonel Barker was surely bent on keeping people out. It was surrounded by high, thick timber walls with one big double gate in the front. Two soldiers in Yankee uniforms swung the gates open to let them through, then pushed them solidly closed again.

After they'd tied their horses to the hitching rail in front of the long, shady front porch, Howard and Blondie herded them inside and down a long hallway to a big office. As they entered, Tad stayed as close by Cam's side as he could. Once Tad had been in Massah Ed's office, and it'd looked sort of like this. Paintings hanging from dark walls, shelves with lots of books and knick-knacks, and a big, curved sword in a fancy silver scabbard hanging on the wall behind the huge desk. But Massah Ed had flowers and pictures of horses and children. This Colonel Barker had pictures of bloody battles, lots of guns, knives and sabers, and fancy papers with swirly writing and gold-embossed seals. Two Yankees in uniform stood guard on either side of the desk.

Seated behind it in a well-cushioned chair was an old man dressed in a much cleaner, nicer uniform than Howard and Blondie. His white hair was slicked down, and wire-rimmed spectacles perched on the end of a nose that looked like a chicken's beak. When he finally glared up at them from his papers, his pale eyes were watery and blood shot, like his Pa's used to look after a night of corn liquor and carousing. More neatly trimmed white hair framed his thin mouth and puffed out around his ears.

Tad pushed in closer to Cam.

After a few moments of just standing there, waiting for someone to say something, Howard finally cleared his throat and spoke up. "We caught this Rebel infiltrator down by the creek, Colonel, sir."

The Colonel leveled those milky eyes on Tad. "Accompanied by his Negro slave, too, I see." The Colonel shifted his eyes up to Cam. "Apparently you don't seem to recognize that we freed these people, Sergeant. Or Lieutenant? Captain? Which is it?"

"It's Mister. My name's Campbell McCool. And the war's over, Colonel. And, yes, I understand what was done by it."

"Well, a declaration of peace does not necessarily settle all accounts, as we can plainly see, now does it, McCool?" The Colonel nodded toward Tad.

"This is Tademus Co." Campbell put a reassuring arm around Tad's shoulder. "He's my ward and friend, not my slave."

Blondie stepped up, sounding anxious to get in his two cents. "He was acting and behaving pretty much like your slave from what we was observin' down by the river."

"Indeed." The Colonel flicked his eyes to Blondie, but quickly returned his glare to Cam. "Your ward, you say? And on whose authority, might I inquire?"

"I have the adoption papers."

The Colonel held out his hand and snapped his fingers. "Well, let's see these papers, Soldier."

Campbell pulled the papers from his jacket pocket and held them out toward the Colonel.

One of his guards rushed to take them from Campbell's hand, and passed them to Barker, then clicked back to standing like a wooden soldier.

After glancing casually at the two pieces of paper, the Colonel dropped them on the desk. "Why, these amount to no more than ownership documents. Does my point begin to register now, Soldier? You see, it just doesn't appear we've resolved this slavery issue at all, does it?"

Tad felt Cam shift his weight uneasily. "So how do you propose that we resolve it, Colonel?"

The Colonel stood abruptly and slammed a hand down on the desk. "You, Soldier, are in no position to be curt with me. I am the commanding officer here, and you have been caught infiltrating my ranks. And with a slave in tow!"

"Yes, it would seem that those are serious charges."

"No, Soldier, grave! Indeed, most grave," the Colonel snarled. "What is your mission?"

"Our destination is Jefferson City." Cam was trying to stay calm, Tad could tell, but he didn't think it was working.

"And your business there?"

"My business there is of a personal nature."

"And your presence here, at this inquisition, is my business. And my business, presently, is that of interrogating a prisoner!" The Colonel's face turned red with rage.

He paused for a moment, sucking in deep breaths, calming himself some. "Now, we can conduct this affair in a civil manner or in a military one. That decision is yours, McCool."

"Seems to me, Colonel, that the commitment has already been made, favoring the military way."

The Colonel addressed one of his guards sharply. "Take the boy to quarters. We'll deal with him later."

Tad felt panic hit him like a fist, knocking the breath out of him. He grabbed Cam's hand and held on for dear life.

"You'll take him nowhere!" Campbell pulled Tad around behind him. Leaning onto the Colonel's desk, coming almost nose to nose, he spoke softly and threateningly. "Colonel, my string's all run out with your little charade. The war is over, and people like you are just gonna have to try and live with that fact."

The Colonel snapped up ram-rod straight and waved at one of the guards. "Follow my order."

When the guard reached out, Tad scooted away. Campbell shoved the man hard back against the desk. Before Tad could open his mouth, the other guard lashed out with his rifle, slamming the butt into the back of Cam's head with a terrible thud, and the Preacherman collapsed to the floor.

Tad heard himself scream. He scrambled toward Cam, but he was grabbed from behind, and a big, sweaty hand clamped down over his mouth. He swung and kicked at every part of his captor that he could reach, but nothing made contact. As he was dragged through the door, his last terrifying sight was of Campbell, unconscious and bleeding on the fancy flowered carpet.

Terror struck him like a thunderbolt. Then the white-hot pain. Campbell gasped and choked on the water streaming over his face, and consciousness flashed back into his brain.

He was kneeling in the mud puddle left by the bucket of water that had been dumped over him, shirtless, and draped over the hitching rail, with his arms tied out spread-eagle. The Colonel was pacing stiffly back and forth in front of him. As his vision cleared, he could make out a young woman behind the Colonel, standing on the porch, clutching a post as if it were her only support.

"You must understand, Soldier." The Colonel picked up as if there had been no break in the conversation. "I've paid a mighty high price in this war."

Breathing shallowly, trying to control the dizziness and nausea, Campbell managed to choke out, "Where's Tad?"

The old man continued as if he hadn't heard. "Now that I've bought my way into it, I'm neither prepared nor am I willing to recognize a couple of broken generals, somewhere in another part of the forest, telling me as to when my duties of war have ended."

"Where is he? Where's Tad?" His own shout set off painful fireworks in his head. "So help me God, if you hurt that boy...."

The Colonel leaned down close to Cam's face, the sour stench of bourbon intensifying the nausea. Quietly, the old man pronounced, "The flesh of my flesh I have sacrificed to the cause of freedom for the Negroes of our land. Your violation of those rights makes you, Soldier, remain as my enemy. And for that, you shall be punished."

Cam yanked against his bindings, desperately trying to free himself. "This is insane!"

"No, Soldier, this is war."

The Colonel stepped back a few paces, then nodded to someone Cam couldn't see. He knew what was coming, and he steeled himself, but he wasn't ready for it.

The first lash burned into his bare back, ripping open flesh.

Teeth clamped tight, eyes squeezed shut, he managed not to cry out. The second lash scoured into the open wound, and he jerked involuntarily. With the third lash, he allowed the scream he could no longer contain, and he stopped counting. Through the red haze, he saw the frowning gaze of the girl clinging to the porch post, and he pleaded silently with her to do something, anything. Surely she couldn't be as deranged as the old man. Maybe she'd look out for Tad. He opened his mouth to speak, but with the next scouring agony, darkness swallowed the pain.

TAD'S JOURNEY

CHAPTER

15

I**T WAS DARK AND HOT** in the coal shed. After they'd pushed him in here and slammed and locked the door, Tad had scrambled around looking for a way out, but there was none. From outside somewhere, he'd heard Campbell scream, and it had send chills through him. They were doing something awful to him, just because he and Cam had been together, and that scared him more than the darkness and the men with guns. What if they killed his Preacherman? Tad had crawled into a corner, cobwebs clinging to his face, and started to sob. He'd told himself he wasn't going to cry, but he couldn't help it. He'd never been more terrified in his whole life. He pulled his knees up tighter to his chest, and swiped a sleeve across his face, coarse coal dust scratching his cheek.

It had been a long time. What if they'd forgotten him? He'd sung every song he could think of, but it scared him even more when he couldn't remember the verses to ones Cam had taught him. He talked to God for a while, but really wasn't sure God could hear him while he was locked up here in the dark. And he practiced the alphabet in his head. Cam would be proud that he could recite the whole thing. Camel... please be alright....

The rattle of a key in the lock woke him out of a light sleep. When the door creaked open, only moonlight spilled in.

Tad stood up from his corner, ready to take on whoever came through the door.

"Come with me, son," a girl's voice whispered.

"Where's Massah Camel?" He used the title out of habit and out of fear. You could never be too sure about who might object to an uppity black boy.

"It's alright. My name's Julie. You just come with me," she urged. "And be very quiet."

The shadow in the long dress hurried across the yard and into the stables, and Tad ran after her, his heart beating like some small, caged animal in his chest. She pushed him toward a buggy that already had a horse in the traces, and one tied to the back.

The girl gave him a little push. "Quickly, jump in and climb under those blankets."

Tad took a step back, panic rising. "But Massah Camel, ma'am, I can't go off and leave him."

"I'm taking you to him, boy," she snapped. "Now hurry and get up there."

He didn't know who she was or what she was doing, but he had no other choice. Like Cam always told him, he had to have faith. He climbed into the back of the buggy and covered himself with the smelly horse blankets as Miss Julie climbed into the driver's seat and took the reins. "Be very still. You'll be with your Massah real soon."

For a long time the buggy bounced over rough roads, rattling his teeth with every rut it hit. All the while Tad argued with his fear, trying to convince himself he was doing the right thing. When they finally stopped, he remained still, until Miss Julie pulled the blankets off him and helped him jump to the ground. She grabbed him by the hand and pulled him up the rickety back stairs of a house, where another lady cracked open the door just wide enough for them to squeeze through.

Julie grabbed the woman's dress sleeve. "Lexxie, did Micah get him here alright?"

"He surely did. That Micah may be a brute, but he's a kind brute." The other lady gestured toward another door. "He's in there, but I wouldn't say he's 'alright'."

Tad knew who they meant. He yanked his hand from Miss Julie's and bolted for the open door. His eyes came to rest on the prone, still form of Campbell lying on a high, frilly canopy bed. Both fear and relief propelled him across the room to the bedside. "Camel, you alright? Camel?"

Campbell lay on his side, unmoving. His shirt was gone, and blood from the awful, deep, gashes on his back dripped dark stains onto the delicate pink and blue flowered coverlet. Tad leaned down closer and whispered, "Camel... it's Tademus. I's here, Camel."

Campbell didn't stir.

The women had followed him into the bedroom. "Has he shown any signs of reviving?" Julie asked her friend.

"No, but Lawd, I wish this man would. Sisterwoman, I don't believe you've been sharing the wealth." The woman called Lexxie shook her head. "Whatever in the world happened to this poor soul?"

"It's not what you may be thinking, Lexxie. But there's no time to explain right now. Bandage him and get a fresh shirt on him, and let's get him downstairs. I've got a carriage down there."

The one called Lexxie came and knelt beside Tad. She had a kind smile and a sweet voice. "Here, son, hold this basin of water while I finish cleaning up these wounds, then you can help us carry him down to Julie's carriage."

"Is he gonna be alright?"

She squeezed his arm. "Of course he will."

With gentle, efficient hands, Miss Lexxie finished washing away the blood, smoothed a pungent salve into the cuts, and then wrapped clean, white bandages all around Cam's middle. Together, they managed to get a shirt onto him, but the whole time, the Preacherman didn't twitch a muscle. Even when the three of them lifted him and carried him down the back steps to the carriage, he never flinched.

"I don't know where to tell you to head-out, son." Miss Julie pushed Tad up onto the driver's seat, handing him Camel's saddlebags and the reins. "But whatever you do, just make sure you keep on traveling away from here."

"Wait, Julie. I know." Lexxie pushed past her and grabbed Tad's hand. "Listen, little boy, you take out northeast of here. Just go down the road in front of the house, here, and leave town by the road leading out. It's just beyond the bank. It'll take you out toward Jefferson City. But before Jeff City, just this side, not more than fifteen or twenty miles from here, you'll come down into a hollow where there's a little white church. You turn right just past the graveyard. About a mile up that road, you should come upon the Manning place. They're real special folks, and they'll help you out. Now, you got all that, son?"

"Yessum." Tad nodded vigorously and repeated the instructions, more for his own sake than hers. Wherever he was taking Camel, it had to be better than here.

"Who're these Mannings?" Julie asked.

"You remember the Manning boy," Lexxie reminded her. "Marler Manning, that handsome, blonde young thing with those green eyes? He used to stop in here every so often."

Miss Julie chuckled. "Now I think you've been hoarding some of the wealth, Lexxie Eden."

Miss Lexxie giggled too. "Oh no, Sisterwoman, it wasn't like that. I run a respectable boarding house here." Then her tone turned serious. "I heard he didn't come back from the war. But he talked about his folks a whole lot. They sounded like real nice people, church-going and all, you know? Anyway, his family was real important to him. I guess that's why I thought about them just now. Doesn't seem to be enough people like that around these days."

Miss Julie turned back to Tad. "Then that's where you head, boy. As fast as you can."

She gave the horse a good swat, and it leapt forward, taking Tad and Cam down the dark road.

The night was as black as ink and heavy with the threat of rain from the thick clouds that hid the moon and stars. Tad knew he was pushing the horse too hard, but all he could think of was Campbell, lying death-like in the back of the carriage, and getting him to someone who could help him. Now that he was out of that coal shed, God could probably hear him, so he started praying. "Lawd, I just know you ain't gonna let Camel die now, is ya? We done come a long, long way together, and he sure works plenty hard for you. And he reads, all the time, from the Good Book. Besides, I just ain't never had nobody the likes of him before, Lawd. I reckon I might not be able to make it if anything was to happen to Camel. Ya sees, Lawd, I needs him. I needs him real bad, and he needs me, too, some…I think. We's just right together somehows, you know, Lawd? And I'd sure be much obliging if you'd just, somehows or other, sees fit to let him stay. We'll sure try and live real good!" The sobs started again, and he didn't try to control them.

Tad reached over and made sure Cam was still secure, pulling the blanket up around his shoulders. "You listening to me, Camel? Can you hear me? You can hear me, I knows you can. You just can't talk right now, but that there's alright. I'm getting you some help, just right on up the road a little piece. We'll be there soon, so you just hold on, Camel, alright? Oh please, Lawd... please." The carriage rattled on through the emptiness of the night, as if the horse understood his fear.

In the darkness, Tad almost missed the turn at the grave-yard. He had to pull the horse up short, and make an awk-ward turn in the rutted road. Miss Lexxie had been right. About a half mile along, the narrow lane opened into a farm yard. On the far side, light filtered out around the curtains of a little two-story house. From the hay loft in the barn to the left, a rooster crowed his arrival.

Tad didn't wait for the horse to stop before he leapt from the carriage seat and ran up the steps to the porch shouting, "Help! Anybody home? Please help!" He hammered on the front door with both fists until it swung inward. "Please help me. Camel's hurt real bad... "

"Settle down, boy." The gray-haired woman frowning down at him was wiping her hands on her apron. "What's the matter?"

"It's Camel, ma'am, he's been hurt real bad, and Miss Lexxie and Miss Julie says that you could help."

The woman squinted at him from behind her wire-rimmed spectacles. "Camel...?"

Tad grabbed her hand and pulled her down the steps toward the carriage. Climbing into the back, he carefully pulled the blanket from around Cam's shoulders. Dark stains spread across the back of his shirt.

The woman gasped. "My goodness, what happened?" Before Tad could answer, she turned and yelled toward the house. "James! James, come quick."

"Ma'am, he's hurt real bad... " Tad knew he was babbling, but he couldn't help it. He'd thought all the jolting over the rough road would wake Camel up, but it hadn't, and he knew that was bad.

Out of the front door came a tall older man dressed in long johns, britches and suspenders, followed by a girl who appeared to be in her teens. Tad repeated his mantra for the newcomers. "Camel's been hurt bad, and they said you might could help...."

The man had already taken charge, jumping into the back of the carriage and pushing Tad to the side. "I'll say he's hurt bad. Mamie, Sudie Anne, help me lift him and get him into the house." The Manning's young daughter, Sudie Anne, all of 15 years old, bore a sweet countenance.

Tad winced at every movement as the three strangers pulled Cam's slack body from the carriage. The man called James lifted him in strong arms, carrying him up the steps and into the house. Tad rushed after them, following them into a bedroom just down the hall to the left. They seemed to have forgotten about him, so he leaned into a corner and kept watch, hugging himself tight to keep from shaking.

The older couple whispered in concerned tones as they cut away the blood-stained shirt and bandages. The girl fetched a pan of water and some sheets, and she and her mother started gently cleaning the deep gashes.

"I'll go fetch Doc Lester," the man told them as he left the room. "This boy needs more help than we can give him."

These people hadn't turned him away and slammed the door in his face. They're helping. They're taking care of Camel. Tad felt like he could breathe again, but he couldn't stop staring at Camel lying so still and quiet on that bed. Cleaning those terrible cuts must've hurt like the devil, but Camel didn't even flinch. Tad thought if he looked away for even a minute, if he stopped hoping and wishing for even a second, Cam would leave him. If he stopped praying, God would take Camel away. All the strength drained from him, and he slid down the wall to sit on the floor in the corner.

"Little boy, are you alright?"

The girl was leaning down in front of him, and she placed a hand on his shoulder. "My name's Sudie Anne. What's yours?"

"Tad, ma'am." He remembered his manners and pushed to his feet. "Tademus Co, of Marion County, Mis'sippi."

"Is he your master?"

"No, ma'am. He's Campbell McCool. He's my friend. My guardian." The word felt odd in his mouth. "Is he gonna be alright?"

The older woman was standing at the bedside, folding the left-over bandages. "My husband has gone for the doctor. If anyone can help your friend here, it'll be Doc Lester."

Tad nodded, not taking his eyes from his Camel.

"Can you tell us what happened to him, Tad?"

Julie and Lexxie had told him to be quiet. It was a dangerous secret. Tad didn't know how far that secret extended, but he didn't want to take any chances. "This man, a ways back, got mad at him..."

"What man? Why was he so mad?"

"I dunno, ma'am, he was just real mad..."

"Alright, Tad. We'll talk about it later. Are you hungry? We were just fixin' to have breakfast."

Tad liked her. She had a warm smile. "No, ma'am. I'd just like to stay right here with Camel, if it's alright with you, ma'am."

"Of course it's alright." She pulled a straight-backed chair over to the bedside. "You come sit right here and let us know if he wakes up."

Tad did as he was told, as the two women left the room.

Since God didn't seem to hear the prayers in his head, he started praying out loud again. It wasn't long before he'd offered God everything within his power to give, if God would just let Camel be alright. He promised not to steal anything ever again, even if he was hungry and cold. He promised not to lie anymore, although sometimes he thought it wasn't really lying, just not telling all the truth. He'd read the Bible every day, as soon as he learned how to read, and he'd never talk back to Camel ever again.

The nice lady—Mamie Manning, she'd introduced herself—had brought him a plate of ham and grits, but he only ate some of it, just to be polite. He hadn't lied when he'd told her he wasn't hungry. He wouldn't be hungry again until Camel woke up... and could share some of this meat with him!

KEEPING THE FAITH

CHAPTER
~ 16 ~

THE SUN HAD COME UP by the time James Manning returned with the doctor, neatly dressed in a dark suit and carrying a large leather satchel. At the doctor's urging, Tad moved out of the way, back into a corner.

The doctor took his time examining Campbell from head to toe, every once in a while making a kind of "hmmm" noise. Finally, he packed all of his instruments back into his bag.

"What do you think, Dr. Lester?" Jim Manning asked.

"In addition to the brutal whipping someone gave him, he's also sustained a severe blow to the back of the head and suffered a concussion. Luckily there doesn't appear to be any damage to the skull itself."

Sudie frowned. "What are his chances?"

"The answer to that, unfortunately, will only come with time." The Doctor removed his spectacles and scrubbed them with his handkerchief. "If the concussion proves to have been only slight, then once out of the coma state, he should begin to recover reasonably satisfactorily, given no other complications. On the other hand. . . ."

Tad didn't understand all those big words, but he understood the tone and the frowns. "Sir. . . Massah Doctor Lestah, sir. . . what if he don't never wake up?"

"Well, if it were to prove to be a major one. . . a major concussion, that is. . . Then it's in the Lord's hands."

So it was still up to God. This white man's doctor was suppose to be smart and educated. He's suppose to have some special potion or magic to make people well again. What good was he if it was still up to God? Tears welled up in Tad's eyes and spilled down his cheeks. He'd gotten good at praying, and he could do it as long as God needed him to.

"Looking at things optimistically, though," the doctor continued, "his reflexes appear to be intact and good."

"Reflexes?" Mrs. Manning asked.

"He has involuntary muscle response to stimulation, as far down, even, as his lower extremities. This provides us a strong indication that there should be no paralysis to fear. There seems to have been no perceptible damage to that portion of the brain at the base of the skull where the blow was administered. What, if anything, will be affected with regards to his memory will only be known in time."

Dr. Lester looked at Mr. Manning, his brows coming together in a frown. "Jim, who could have been responsible for this assault?"

"We haven't been able to get anything out of the boy," Mrs. Manning told them. "He's obviously terrified."

"Yes, he could be fearful of reprisals," the doctor agreed. "Well, the main thing that you must do now is keep him as comfortable as you can and, if at all possible, get some nourishment into him. Try getting some chicken broth or the like down him. He'll need all the strength he can muster. Maybe even more importantly, he's going to need the will to live."

Closing his bag and heading for the door, Dr. Lester added, "I'd like to see his fever break, too. Keep bathing him all over with cool, wet towels. There's really nothing more that can be done for him right now, by any of us. He'll need a far stronger healing hand upon him than we can provide. I'll be back out in a day or two, but send for me if he shows any signs of coming around before then."

After everyone had left the room, Tad pushed his chair back up next to the bed and started praying again. "You heard that Dr. Lester, God. It's all up to you now. If there's something else you be needin' from me, I'd be obliged if you'd let me know."

Tad had watched the patch of sunlight crawl across the quilt covering Camel, then fade and disappear, leaving the room in deep shadows, then return again the next morning to make the same slow trip. But he hadn't kept track of how many times that had happened. Mrs. Manning or Sudie would bring him food, and he'd eat because he knew he had to. They brought broth and warm, soft cereal and showed him how to prop extra pillows behind the still-unconscious Cam, and carefully feed him. They brought supplies of cool water and wet towels, and bathed his face and his body to try to ease the fever. They'd laid a pallet for Tad beside the bed, but he couldn't see his Camel from there, so he mostly stayed sitting in the chair.

This bedroom had belonged to someone once. It still had that warm, lived-in feeling. The windows were hung with clean curtains, and a brightly colored braided rug covered the floor. The quilt covering Cam was worn with years of loving use. The few things sitting on top of the dresser belonged to a man—a comb and brush, a pair of cuff links, and a bow tie—as if they'd just been left there the night before, when their owner came home from a party. A small stack of little cards with photographs on them sat to one side—the kind white folk left behind when they came calling. Tad hadn't dare look through them, but the top one was of a pretty girl with long, blonde hair.

Early one evening, Miss Sudie had come in and instead of taking away the empty soup bowl, she'd settled into the arm chair across the bed from him and opened a book in her lap. "Do you mind if I sit with you a while, Tad?"

Tad only shook his head. It wasn't his place to tell her what she could do in her own house.

"Can you read, Tad?"

"No, ma'am. Camel been trying to learn me how, though, so's I can read the Good Book."

"An excellent ambition. I've heard you telling him stories. Do you think he can hear you?"

"Yes, ma'am. I do."

He'd spent hours telling Camel the stories his Ma used to tell him when he was little. He'd talked about all his friends back on Massah Ed's plantation and how he missed them, and about Young Massah and all his lady friends, and about that time Ol' Barney, the head field slave, had let him ride the mule that pulled the plow, but then the mule got stung by a bee. He'd laughed at the memory of that one himself.

That evening Miss Sudie had read to him and Camel from her book, a story about an orphan boy about his age who dreamed of being important and rich one day, starting out as a blacksmith. Tad had only heard part of the story before his thoughts drifted away, back to Camel.

He and God had gotten to know each other real well during these long days, although Tad was the one who did most of the talking. A couple of times in the dark of night though, he'd thought he heard God answering, but he couldn't be sure.

This new day began as the others had, with the familiar stream of sunlight waking him from a light sleep, and Miss Sudie bringing in breakfast before beginning her morning chores.

"I knows you's gettin' better, Camel. You ain't burning up with fever like you was, and your color's lookin' real good." Tad smiled at his own weak joke as he spooned the last of the chicken broth into Camel's mouth.

He set the empty bowl on the bedside table and reached behind Cam to pull out the extra pillows that had been propping him up when he thought he heard Cam make a noise. Tad stared at him for a long minute, about deciding it had been his imagination, when he saw Cam's lips first part then move slightly.

Tad leaned in close, his ear next to Cam's mouth. "I's here, Camel. It's me, ol' Tademus..."

It was just a breath against his ear, "...of...Marion Coun...tee...Mis...sippee...?"

"Camel! CAMEL!!" Tad leapt to his feet, his heart nearly bursting from his chest. "You's awake! You's back!" Energy rushed from him in a flood, and he ran back and forth around the room, unable to contain it, shouting so loud his throat hurt. "Camel! Camel! Camel's awake!"

Mrs. Manning appeared at the door, eyes wide. "My goodness, Tademus, what happened?"

"He woke up, Miz Manning! Camel's gonna be okay."

"Oh my..."

Tad joined her as she sat on the edge of the bed and gently pushed a lock of hair back off Cam's forehead. His eyes opened a slit, and he tried again to speak, his lips moving silently.

"It's alright, son, you're safe now," Miz Manning soothed. "You've come back to us."

Tad looked up at the ceiling and shouted a joyful "Hallelujah!" God had listened!!! God had decided to let his Camel stay.

RESURRECTION

photography by BB

CHAPTER

17

THE ROOM WAS STILL DARK when he opened his eyes, but the smell of ham frying and coffee boiling made his stomach grumble. Laying on the soft feather bed in the peaceful pre-dawn, the only noise being the occasional clink of a pot from the kitchen, Campbell realized this was the first time he'd awakened without a headache. And he was famished. Mamie, Sudie Anne, and Tad had taken turns feeding him small meals and helping him with the necessities, but he'd spent most of the last three days just sleeping. This morning he needed to get up and move. And eat.

He swung his legs to the floor and sat up slowly, letting his body get its bearings, then he stood, holding onto the bedside table until he was sure his balance wouldn't betray him. When he lit the oil lamp on the dresser, it gave the room the warm, comforting glow he had come to cherish over the last few days.

In the wardrobe next to the window, he found his clothes hung neatly. As he pulled on his old, worn uniform pants, he discovered that they'd been laundered and mended. A loose button had been reattached, and the tear near the cuff was neatly stitched up. His shirt smelled of strong soap, but all the scrubbing in the world wasn't going to remove the stains. Blood stains. He wondered again how they'd gotten there, and whose blood it was.

It was amazingly frustrating. Cam knew Tademus as the freed slave boy who'd been looking for his father. Tad had filled him in about how that search had turned out, and about how Cam had legally adopted him. But even then his memories of those weeks were only shadows of dreams with the occasional vivid flare of clarity. He knew he'd been a Confederate doctor, but again, his memories of the war stopped somewhere in a field hospital in Mississippi, his home state. The rest was a gray, misty void with disturbing shadows floating through it, from which he could make no coherent picture. Sometimes, when one of those shadows would come close, he'd try to grab it and hold onto it, but it always scooted just out of his grasp. He was trying to accept the reality that he may never regain his past. But now it was time to start living in the present.

Not wanting to startle the women as they prepared breakfast, Campbell stood quietly at the kitchen door for a moment, watching them work. The mother and daughter moved efficiently around the spacious kitchen, and each other, adding a log to the fire, giving a boiling pot a stir, repeating the dance they'd done together for a lifetime.

Mamie casually backhanded a loose strand of salt-and-pepper hair off of her face as she flipped a slice of ham in the skillet. She had the small, spare frame of a woman who'd spent a lifetime working as hard as her menfolk to take care of her family, but she was not the kind to consider any of it a hardship. Her work was a joy to her, and that joy lit her whole face, and animated her every move.

Although dressed in men's coveralls that had obviously been cut down and taken in to fit her petite stature, Sudie Anne would never be mistaken for a boy. She'd taken on many of the chores a young man should have been doing around the farm, but still managed to move with a sway and grace that must've driven the boys crazy. This morning she had her yellow hair pulled into a long braid down her back, and her face glowed with the heat of the stove and the bright freshness of youth.

When she saw him standing, leaning in the doorway, she rushed to him, grabbing his arm in support. "Campbell, should you be out of bed?"

He straightened to reinforce the fact that he could stand on his own two feet. "I believe it's time I start making myself useful around here."

"Are you sure you're up to it?" Even Mamie's frown was motherly. "I was just about to bring you some breakfast."

"The wonderful aromas have pulled me from my sick-bed, and if it's all the same to you, ma'am, I'd be honored if I could join you all at your breakfast table this morning."

Mamie laughed out loud. "Of course you can! It's good to have you finally among us."

Cam took a seat at the long plank table, and after a few minutes, Jim came downstairs to join him. When Tad came through the back door with the basket of eggs he'd just collected, he almost spilled them in his excitement to see Cam up and dressed.

"'Bout time you was stoppin' your lallygaggin' and gettin' yourse'f movin'. You needs to be earnin' your keep around here like the rest of us." Tad's wide grin contradicted his annoyance.

"Do you think you're up to it?" Jim asked.

"I might not be able to clear the north 40 quite yet, but Tad's right. I need to get started paying you folks back for all your kindness."

"Nonsense." Mamie set a platter of scrambled eggs in the middle of the table. "The only thing you need to do is get better."

"Yes, ma'am," Cam agreed, hiding a smile. For all her gentle goodness, he felt that Mamie Manning would be a fearsome woman to disobey.

After saying grace, they all dug into the hearty breakfast and shared their various plans for the day. This all feels so right, Cam thought. His own upbringing must've been much like this. But there were so many empty spaces in his head where memories should be.

At first Cam found that he tired easily. A morning of helping Tad with his chores around the farmyard or driving into town for supplies with Mamie would leave him exhausted, barely able to stand. Gradually, over several weeks of good meals and a lot of rest, with the Manning women doting over him like nursemaids, he'd regained his strength, all the while with Tademus reminding him that he shouldn't be getting soft and lazy. Life settled into a steady, thrumming routine of fence mending and tool mending, planting and harvesting, fattening hogs and hauling grain for market.

The close of each day was Tad's favorite time, and Cam had to admit that it was his, as well. After supper, when the kitchen was cleaned up and all the chores were done, the family gathered in the sitting room around the fireplace, with the light from the fire augmented by glowing oil lanterns, strategically placed about the room.

Mamie pulled out her sewing basket, sometimes having mending to catch up on, sometimes stitching on elaborate, colorful pieces of decorative needlework. Several of her samplers hung in the bedrooms, but she said that mostly she gave them away to friends.

Sudie Anne always sat in her special rocker next to a lamp with her latest adventure novel open in her lap. She'd told him once that someday she hoped to see for herself all the far-away, magical places she read about.

At a table at the far side of the room, Tad would badger Cam into a game or two of checkers or dominoes, and in actuality, it didn't take much badgering. Tad had become a formidable opponent in both games. Every now and then, Cam could con Tad into the more challenging game of chess, confident that soon the boy would be challenging his 'chess master' in that competition, as well. Campbell looked, indeed, to the time when the line between 'master' and 'subservient' was completely blurred.

Jim always went straight to the mantle and reached up to fetch his brown bottle of Garrett snuff. He would stand there by the fireplace, with his head titled back as he filled a healthy load of the ground-up tobacco inside his lower lip between teeth and gum. Then he would amble over to relax in his cowhide-bottomed and backed rocking chair to begin gently rocking. He would study the newspaper, catching up on stock and grain prices as well as the news, and he'd soon have worked up a good, juicy tobacco spit.

At this point, Tad would lose interest in their board game, focusing on Jim in anticipation of which forward rocking motion he might decide to use to take a shot at hitting the fireplace with a squirt of his tobacco juice. The try would eventually come, but invariably the effort would fall short.

Mamie would always heave a sigh and shake her head. "I reckon we'll just have to move the fireplace closer to Jim."

Every time, Tademus would practically fall out of his chair laughing. He never tired of the ritual. And Jim never tired of the appreciative audience. He especially enjoyed telling of his fetching his bride, Mamie Baker, out of some damn Yankee's clutches up in Indiana and bringing her down South. He proudly wore his cocked eye which had been awarded him in a knife-fight while defending the honor of his Yankee gal he'd made Mamie Baker Manning. As a matter of fact,

Jim was grown before he realized that damnYankees was two words. He had a mental library of tall tales and legends that never failed to entertain them all, although Cam was sure Mamie and Sudie had heard most of them many times before. They would demonstrate this fact by raising one hand if they'd heard the story once and both hands if twice. Jim would acknowledge with, "Yeah, maybe, but I'm gonna tell it again because it gets better with each telling."

Jim would sit there, rocking, with his lower lip bulging with the tobacco snuff and look over at Tad with a twinkle in his eye. "It's a sin to smoke, you know, Tad."

Tad knew his part in this little drama. "How comes you sayin' that, Massah James, when there you sits with your mouth full of snuff?"

"Well, that's what I'm talking about, son. Why, now don't you know that it's a downright sin to burn anything that tastes this good?"

Tad's boyish laughter would fill the room to the rafters, and none of them ever tired of that.

Life was good. The family was whole again.

WHILE CULTIVATING
THE SOUL

CHAPTER
18

SUMMER HAD SPED BY in a haze and suddenly August was gone, and the days and nights were cooling off. This morning, the dust of the newly plowed soil caught on a freshening westerly breeze that brought with it the smell of autumn and drying leaves, and promised a much-needed rain for the new winter cotton crop. Watching the clouds gather and wanting to get finished before the storm rolled in, Campbell encouraged Ol' Prince the mule with an extra slap of the reins.

When the plow blade hit a rock, the jolt went all the way to his shoulders. He took the opportunity to pull the bandana from around his neck and wipe his face with it before untangling himself from the reins and going to shove the chunk of granite out of the way.

"Here, let me give you a hand with that." Jim Manning had left his own plow three rows over and come to stoop beside Cam, adding his weight to roll the rock aside. "If this field would grow cotton the same way it grows rocks, we'd be richer than Solomon."

Cam brushed the rich, dark soil from his hands and stood, stretching the kinks out of his back. "Ain't that the truth. They do seem to sprout like weeds."

Tad's sharp whistle from under the elm at the south edge of the field got their attention, and the thought of the cool water the boy had hauled out on the back of the hand cart reminded Cam just how hot and thirsty he really was. He smiled and slapped Jim on the back, sending up a small cloud of dust. "Looks like we've been given a reprieve anyway." They both unhitched their mules from the plows and led them over to join Tad under the tree.

While the mules enjoyed the buckets of water Tad had brought for them, Cam and Jim slumped into the grass against the tree, swilling from their jugs.

When Cam looked around, Tad had run off toward the creek where it emerged from the woodlands to their west, dragging the cart behind him. After a few minutes, he returned with a ripe, round watermelon loaded in the back of the cart. "I's had this ol' melon chillin' in that creek all mornin'," he announced. "Should be jest 'bout done by now."

A wide grin split Jim's ruddy features as he got to his feet. "So that's what's been happenin' to all my melons in that south patch. I knew that crop started off with more fruit on the vine." He lifted the shiny wet melon from the back of the cart and gave it a thump with his knuckles. "Well at least let me share this one with you boys. Nothing eases a man's plowing thirst on a hot day like a juicy melon, but you boys already know that, don't you?"

Lifting the melon above his head, Jim then heaved it to the ground where it smashed into several large chunks. He picked up one of the larger pieces, dug his fingers into the sweet, dripping red innards, and slurped it from his hand. "Dig in, boys, before I eat it all."

It didn't take them long to clean all the sticky goodness from every piece of rind, until there was nothing left but the seeds scattered around from where they'd spit them at each other, and the bees venturing in to harvest some of the bounty. Settling back against the tree, Jim used some of the water from a jug to rinse the melon juice from his hands.

Worry still creased his sun-browned brow as he looked at Campbell. "You're not having any more of those headaches, are you?"

"No, sir," Cam reassured him with a smile. "Not for a while. Still don't remember much before waking up in your front room, though."

Cam looked over at the man sitting next to him, leaning back against the sturdy elm trunk. Tall, wiry, and strong from a lifetime of working the land, gray and slightly balding, James Manning had warm, dark eyes, a quick smile, and a devout and loving heart. Whatever Cam had done in his previous life, it couldn't have been all bad, if it had earned him the reward of having this man, these people, as friends.

Tad had remained unusually quiet, standing and staring out at the partially plowed field. "That all the farther you two got after all this time?" he finally blurted.

By now, Cam was used to taking the bait. "And just how far should we have gotten?"

"Well, if Ol' Barney was here, he'd a had y'all starting on the next field by now. He just never stood for no lazybones. Y'all's just not doing it right."

"Is that so? And you're the expert on field plowing now?" A smile creased Jim's face. He'd learned to play this game, too.

Tad squared his shoulders and placed his hands resolutely on his hips. "I done my share back in the day..."

Jim exchanged a quick glance with Cam. "What do you think, Dr. McCool?"

"Why, I think young Master Co is about old enough to shoulder his share of the plowing chores, don't you?"

Tad swung around to look at them with wide eyes.

"I do," Jim agreed, pushing to his feet. "Let's hitch 'em up and get the rest of this field done."

Cam untied his mule and held the reins out to Tad, who just stared at them for a moment before tentatively taking them into his small hands. As Tad headed out across the loose furrows, the mule stood his ground, refusing to leave his water bucket.

"C'mon you stubborn ol' swayback," Tad scolded. "We's gots work to do." After a couple of hard tugs, the mule slowly followed Tad out to the plow, along with Cam and Jim.

Cam was impressed at how deftly Tad hitched up the plow, as if he'd done it many times before. Perhaps he'd been a more experienced field slave than his age would have suggested. Tad positioned himself between the plow's handles, looped the reins around his middle, gave the old mule a slap with the leather, and a shout of "git up!" Ol' Prince immediately headed straight across the newly dug furrows, in the direction of the barn and his stall, pulling a struggling Tad along with him. Tad's shouts of "whoa!" and "gee!" were having no affect.

Cam stifled a laugh, but when the mule started to trot, he rushed to intervene, running after the errant animal, grabbing the halter, and yanking him to a stop. "You alright, Tad?"

The boy had pulled back on the reins with all his strength, at least able to stay on his feet. Now he righted himself and looked back at the extra, cock-eyed channel he'd gouged across the otherwise symmetrical field. "He do have a bit of ornery to him, don't he?"

Jim had caught up with them and was holding onto the other side of the harness. "That's a darned nice deep furrow you plowed there, young man. We'll just have to call that one Tademus' Row."

"...Meshach and Abednego," Cam chimed in.

Tad beamed at being the center of their jousting. This must be what freedom AND belonging felt like.

Cam knew for sure that in order to deserve this, he must've done something miraculous back in that other life he couldn't remember.

CHUNK IT IN
BEAVER DAM

CHAPTER

19

SUNDAY MORNINGS BEGAN before dawn, just as every other morning began, with a hearty family breakfast. Even though the Sabbath was suppose to be a day of rest, on a working farm the cows still needed milking and the eggs needed gathering, chickens and hogs needed to be fed, all before it was time to head out to services at the New Hope Community Church, just a mile down the road. Cam looked forward to raising his voice in praise with the rest of the congregation, and to the elderly Pastor Parker's inspiring, though sometimes long-winded messages. They always seemed to reflect the new hope that the church's name promised. And Cam always left the church with an overwhelming desire to be able to do what Pastor Parker did, to bring the Word of God to people, to give them new hope and new life. Maybe one day he could preach from that pulpit, too... or one just like it.

Jim pushed his empty breakfast plate aside and cleared his throat, breaking Cam's reverie. "Campbell, after the morning chores, Mamie and I would like for you to come with us into the back room."

"Jim and I have talked about this, Campbell, and even prayed about it for quite some time, now," Mamie added. "And we've reached this decision."

There was a seriousness to Jim's frown and a hitch in Mamie's voice that made Cam uneasy. He turned to Sudie Anne, but she wouldn't look him in the eye. "And you, young lady, are you a part of this conspiracy?"

"Yes, I'm a part of it," Sadie Anne confided, "but I would add, lest you set about your affairs this morning carrying a heavy heart of dread, that the purpose of this family conference is, after all, a pleasant one."

"Well, that lightens my load a bit. There did seem to be a certain seriousness prevailing." Despite Sudie's reassurances, Cam still felt the heavy weight in the air.

"Oh, it's serious, all right," Sudie Anne was quick to qualify. "But 'happy' serious, not 'sad' serious."

"Well, then, on that note of encouragement, I reckon I might just sneak through the morning."

"Well, indeed." Jim rose from his chair, bringing an end to the conversation. "You two kids, as well as Mamie and young Tademus over there, can all keep your legs under this table if you've a mind to, but may I point out that there's a whole lot of 'sneaking through' left to this morning, if we don't intend to be late for preaching, that is. So I'd best be getting on with my work, leaving that word to the wise."

Cam followed Jim's lead, giving Tad an encouraging nudge on the arm. "Come on, little buddy, why don't we play it smart."

As he and Tad followed Jim out of the house, Tad pulled at his sleeve. "What you think Miss Sudie mean by 'happy' serious? That don't make no sense."

Cam was thinking the same thing. "I guess we'll just have to wait and see."

Campbell went about his Sunday morning routine lost in thought over the odd tone at the breakfast table. The 'back room' provided him with his only clue, but it wasn't much of one. It was a room he'd never been in. The door was always kept closed. Cam had actually never thought much about it, and simply presumed it was used for storing things like Mamie's and Sudie's preserves, or the winter clothes. He'd never had reason to speculate about it until now.

When Cam finished herding the heifers out into the pasture and spreading hay for them, the sun was already high. On his way back to the house, he poked his head into the hen house where Tad should have been collecting eggs, but only the rooster greeted him. When he checked, he found all the eggs still hiding under the hens. It wasn't like Tad to shirk his chores.

Grabbing a basket, Cam quickly gathered up enough eggs to fill it, only getting pecked a couple of times by irate hens not use to his large, clumsy hands, then he headed for the house.

"Cam, is that you?" Jim called from that back room as Cam stepped into the kitchen to set down the basket.

"Yeah, Jim," Campbell called back as he started on down the hallway. The door to the room was already opened, and Jim and Mamie stood over an open trunk on the opposite wall.

Cam stopped in the doorway. "Have either of you seen Tademus? That boy seems to have overlooked some of his chores this morning or, at least, he overlooked some of the eggs, and the hens were letting me know that it's not my hand they're accustomed to having reach under them."

"We haven't seen him around since breakfast, that I can recall right off hand," Mamie replied.

"Well, chances are good he's occupying himself with some all important business somewhere," Cam smiled, hoping to lighten the somber mood that seemed to have returned.

"I think I saw him ambling down toward Beaver Dam earlier," Sudie Anne mentioned as she joined Cam in the doorway.

"I hope he didn't have a fishing pole over his shoulder, forgetting it's Sunday..."

"You two come on in." With a wave of his hand, Jim motioned them into the room, and they walked over to where Jim and Mamie stood by the open trunk.

Mamie reached down and pulled out a dark linen suit, complete with vest, and a crisp white shirt. "Campbell, Jim, Sudie Anne, and I have discussed this and have thought about it and prayed about it, as we told you at breakfast, and we want you to have these clothes."

Mamie's voice cracked, and when she reached for her handkerchief, Jim continue for her. "They belonged to our boy, Campbell. Marler didn't come back to us after the war. He was felled in the fighting at Mobile Bay there near the end." He took a deep breath as he lovingly fingered the fine fabric of the suit jacket. "Our losing Marler settled a sorrow over this family that somehow we've not been able to ease very much."

Mamie dabbed at her wet eyes with the lace hanky. "Your coming into our lives has meant more to us than we could have you understand, son."

She'd called him 'son'. It was the first time that either she or Jim had done that, and it was clear that she had done so intentionally. He felt a surge of love course through his body.

"None of this is to say that we feel anybody could ever take the place of our Marler," Jim resumed. "He was a real fine boy, none finer around these parts, or anywhere else, I reckon. But he had some real strong convictions about the right and the wrong of things, you understand. And it was because of this, he felt it to be his duty to answer his country's call to war. It saddened us, Campbell, it saddened us all real bad that we lost our boy to that war, but... well... the Almighty, He'd seen fit to share him with us for twenty-two years, and for those years we're grateful. But He's called him home now to be with Him, and the rest of us still have more life to serve, yet..."

"We want you to have these clothes, Campbell." Mamie extended the suit of clothes out to Cam. "We'd be privileged to see you claim them as your own and wear them. You and that boy Tademus have brought a lot of life back into this family and a lot of joy. You've taken a very special place among us and in our hearts."

As Campbell accepted the clothes, Mamie leaned up, kissing him on the cheek. Jim extended his hand to shake Campbell's. "Thank you, son. We thank you a whole lot."

Sudie Anne put her arms around Campbell's waist in a tight hug. Cam grabbed a shallow breath against the sudden onslaught of emotion and found his voice. "I don't know what to say... I thank you. I thank you all very much, and I'm honored... very honored, indeed."

Cam ran his hand across the jacket's lapel and fingered the tie hanging loose from the collar of the shirt. Somewhere deep inside that dark part of his brain, an image stirred and flickered, then disappeared. It felt like an important image, but it was gone before he could get a hold of it.

"Now, then." Jim clapped his hands, calling an end to the gathering. "Let's see you wearing those clothes, and let's all get dressed for church before we're late."

"And best you be running down that little Tad, lest he gets left behind," Mamie added.

As Sudie Anne had suggested, Campbell found Tademus down at Beaver Dam, the spot on the creek where the water rushed over a large rock formation. The boy sat perched up on a boulder overlooking the falls, tossing small stones into the water and watching them disappear into the torrent.

Cam eased himself onto the rock next to Tad. "You best be getting a move on, m'lad, if we're gonna get to preachin' service on time." When Tad didn't even look up at him, Cam gathered up his own handful of pebbles and joined in silently casting them into the rapids.

Finally, Tad stopped throwing rocks and just stared into the churning water. "If ya wanna get rid of something forever, Massah James say all ya gotta do is just chunk it into Beaver Dam, and it be gone."

"That's the way it goes, does it?" Cam tossed another stone.

"When somethin' make Massah James mad, like the other day whilst he was hoein', and the handle kept on a comin' outta the hoe, he say 'I'm gonna chunk this damn thing in Beaver Dam and get shut of it forever!' He say there be a kinda way the deep water way down under there just pull anything you throw in it right on down to the bottom, then take it along and you never have to see it no more."

"An undertow."

Tad threw a dozen more stones before he spoke again. "That what they wanna do with me, Camel? Get shut of me in Beaver Dam?"

"What are you talking about, Tademus?"

"I heard them at breakfast saying as how they had something to talk to you about. Is that there whys they couldn't talk right then, because they didn't want me to hear? That why they didn't say nothin' 'bout wantin' to talk to me, too? They just wanna talk to you? They's wantin' me just to be a gettin' on down the road, does they?"

Campbell leaned back on one elbow. "Oh, I see. And you figure what they had to say to me was that they wanted you to leave, huh? That they were ready just to chunk you into Beaver Dam and get rid of you forever. Is that what's been preying on your mind?"

Plop went another rock into the swirling water.

"My, my, that sure is a whole powerful heap of thinking for you to be crowding into your head." Campbell grinned, but Tad's eyes were still on the waterfall. "And this Beaver Dam theory of yours—why, Tad, I do believe I recognize traces of the philosopher and poet in you."

When Tad reached up to swipe a tear from his face, Cam realized that making light of the matter wasn't helping. "No, Tad. You've misinterpreted it all. You've misunderstood. That was not the reason the Mannings wanted to talk to me. That wasn't the purpose they had in mind at all."

Tad sniffled and looked up at Cam with a frown.

"What they wanted to see me about, Tad, was to give me some new Sunday-go-to-meeting clothes. You see? It was nothing like what you were thinking at all. So you just get all those thoughts outta your head, and chunk them right into Beaver Dam!"

"You telling the truth, Camel?" The frown didn't quite disappear.

"The truth, Tademus. I guess about everybody's getting plum tired by now of having to look at me in these soldier pants of mine." Images flared in his mind again, this time of deft, gentle fingers unbuttoning those pants, of golden hair in ringlets, and the sensual feel of satin skin. And a beach covered with craters, and dead bodies of men and horses. They flashed and then faded, leaving him vaguely dizzy.

Tad had jumped up from the rock and was pulling at his sleeve. "Well, come on, Camel! Let's us go and see you in these here new clothes so's we can get on over to the church-house. I betcha I's just bound to laugh! Why I is already, just thinkin' about it!"

Tad's new enthusiasm pulled Cam back to reality. He stood too, and putting his arm around the boy's shoulders, they headed back through the woods, toward the house.

But this time the images didn't entirely disappear. They lingered at the edges of his mind, like smoke from a distant fire. These were important things that he needed to remember. He looked down at the boy walking at his side. "Did you ever hear me mention anything about Mobile Bay, Tad?"

REVELATION

CHAPTER
～ 20 ～

THE HYMN COULD EASILY BE HEARD over the buck-board's creaking wheels as they crunched over the gravel road. The pump-organ sounds and the voices of the congregation echoed joyfully through the hills surrounding the natural hollow in which the New Hope Community Church nestled, and they grew louder as Jim reined into the church yard and brought the horse to a halt. The melodious organ sounds could only be coming from Steve Russell, the Pleasant Grove community's talented young organist.

"Come Thou fount of every blessing; tune my heart to sing Thy grace. Streams of mercy, never ceasing, call for songs of loudest praise. Teach me some melodious sonnet, sung by flaming tongues above. Praise the mount, I'm fixed upon it—mount of Thy redeeming love".

The hymn was coming to a close, and the congregation was being seated again as the Mannings, Campbell, and Tademus entered the little white frame church. Jim, Mamie, and Sudie Anne headed on down the center aisle to occupy their customary pew toward the front, but Cam remained with Tad in the rear of the sanctuary, stepping over with him as they took their seats, joining the blacks in the 'Negro' section. Cam nodded and whispered greetings to the families already seated who moved to make room for them, and Tad quickly scooted over to sit next to his new friend Samuel whose family were share-croppers of the Mannings on a small plot of land nearby. They only got to see each other on Sundays. When the boys started to giggle, Cam reached over and gave Tad a gentle swat on the knee as a reminder of where they were.

A little stooped and doddering, Pastor Parker approached the pulpit and placed his Bible on it, then lifted his face to his congregation. "My sermon this morning, dear friends and visitors," the Pastor began, "is entitled 'My Brother's Keeper', and I have chosen to draw, as my text, from the Holy Scriptures: Genesis, chapter four, verses nine through sixteen. I invite you to join with me now in this reading of His holy word.

"And the Lord said unto Cain, where is Abel thy brother? And he said, I know not; am I my brother's keeper? And He said, What hast thou done? The voice of thy brother's blood crieth unto me from the ground. And now art thou cursed from the earth, which has opened her mouth to receive thy brother's blood from thy hand. When thou tillest the ground, it shall not henceforth yield unto thee her strength; a fugitive and vagabond shalt thou be in the earth. And Cain said unto the Lord, my punishment is greater than I can bear. Behold, thou hast driven me out this day from the face of the earth; and from thy face shall I be hid; and I shall be a fugitive and a vagabond in the earth; and it shall come to pass, that every one that findeth me shall slay me. And the Lord said unto him, Therefore whosoever slayeth Cain, vengeance shall be taken on him sevenfold. And the Lord set a mark upon Cain, lest any finding him should kill him. And Cain went out from the presence of the Lord, and dwelt in the land of Nod, on the East of Eden."

Cam closed his eyes as he listened. Pastor Parker was probably well past 70, but he still had the strong voice of a man used to raising it in praise. Cam knew this passage by heart, and found himself mouthing the words as the Pastor spoke.

"And now art thou cursed from the earth, which has opened her mouth to receive thy brother's blood from thy hand." With a suddenness like a blow to the head, the scene erupted within his mind so vividly that he felt as though he were still there, kneeling next to the boy he'd just shot, watching his life drain from the terrible wound, and from his young eyes. The heat of the morning, the chaffing of his wet, gritty clothes as he dug the grave. The overwhelming uselessness of it all. The vow he'd made to himself that he'd find the boy's family and explain somehow, apologize, try to make things right, although it had felt like nothing would ever be right again. The tintype, with the identifying writing on the back—the formal portrait of the boy with his parents and sister, all dressed in their Sunday best. He opened his eyes to find himself staring down at the very jacket and vest the boy had been wearing when that photograph was taken. The walls closed in on him, all the air rushed from the room, the droning voice of the pastor muddled into white noise, and the room tilted...

"Campbell, Campbell... son... son, are you alright?"

"Fetch another cold rag, Sudie."

"Here's some more water, Miz Mamie."

The voices around him grew louder, until they started making sense. He was lying on something hard, and there was a crowd hovering over him.

"I believe he's beginning to come around," someone said.

As Cam opened his eyes, he found he was lying on a picnic table, one of many scattered around the meadow behind the church. The smell of fried chicken and freshly baked bread was heavy in the air. After church service, dinner-on-the-ground festivities were underway. He remembered now. He knew.

"Son, are you feeling better?" Jim was sitting on the bench to his left.

Mamie was standing behind her husband. "You must've gotten too hot, Campbell."

"Well, we could all use something to eat," Sudie suggested. "Camel...?"

On Cam's right, kneeling on the picnic bench, Tademus frowned down at him. Cam attempted what he hoped was a reassuring smile. "Yeah, I'm alright. I think."

As he tried to push up on an elbow, Jim leaned over to help him sit up, and handed him a cup of water. "Here, you should drink something cool."

The water felt good on his dry throat. "I'm sorry about that. I don't know what happened..." But he couldn't finish the thought. He did know. In crushing, suffocating, horrific detail, he remembered the secret his mind had been trying to hide from him. And now he had to find some way to explain his deed to these loving, giving people whom he'd come to cherish. How do you go about breaking the hearts of people you love as family?

Cam could see the concern in their eyes. Over the next few days, Jim had tried to convince him to sleep later in the mornings, assuring him that not all the chores had to be done by noon. Mamie practically forced him to take extra helpings at meals. Tademus took every opportunity to cling to him, as if afraid he were about to disappear in a cloud of smoke. So Cam did his best to put on a happy-go-lucky face, knowing he really wasn't fooling anyone.

While he shaved in the morning, while he worked alone in the fields, or rubbed down Ol' Prince in the afternoon, and especially on his knees at night, before crawling into bed, physically and mentally exhausted, he prayed.

'Trust in the Lord with all thine heart and lean not unto thine own understanding'. He knew the truth of that and believed it with all his heart, but God was truly testing him. No matter which way he twisted the facts in his mind, there was no way to spare these undeserving, God-fearing people the anguish they'd have to endure. And it was all because of him and his violent, thoughtless actions. He deserved whatever trial God saw fit to burden him with, but certainly the Mannings had done nothing to deserve this. So he continued to talk with God, and continued to hope that God would answer him.

At dinner on Wednesday night, as Cam forced down his third piece of fried chicken, he'd lost track of what Mamie was saying about the Wainwrights' new baby. It had become so hard to concentrate, his mind never moving far from his awful dilemma.

Sudie's hand on his arm got his attention. "It'll be fun, Cam. It's the biggest fair of its kind anywhere. The whole county practically shuts down for the week, and everybody goes."

"Can I go?" Tad bounced in his chair.

Sudie was bubbling with excitement, too. "Of course you can go! I bet you'd do real good in the hog-tying contest. You're quicker at catching those squealing little piglets than anybody I've ever seen. There're all kinds of contests. Mama always wins with her strawberry preserves, and I'm entering that sampler I finished stitching on last Spring. There's music and dancing and food, and on the last night, there's fireworks..."

"Of course we'll go, Sudie." Her father patted her hand, allowing her to take a breath. "Have we ever missed a year?"

But Sudie hadn't yet spent all her ebullience. "We should stay the whole week this year, Poppa. Campbell could really use the rest and relaxation, and I'm sure young Samuel could come take care of all the necessary chores for us while we're away. Please, Poppa? Please!"

Jim and Mamie exchanged that kind of silent communication only old married couples knew, and the smile gave away Jim's decision. "That actually sounds like a wonderful plan. We'll head over there on Saturday afternoon. You boys are in for a treat."

Although it didn't seem to be the sign from God that Cam had been praying for, it would indeed be a distraction. That was something he could sorely use. And God did move in mysterious ways.

TOO LONG AT THE FAIR

CHAPTER

21

THE FAIR HAD ITS ROOTS back a half-century earlier, when the first three families built their cabins in a secluded meadow five miles west of Jefferson City. It was established as a tranquil, verdant retreat from daily drudgery and the summer heat. But over the years, as more and more families added their own cabins to the settlement, the commune grew, as did the recreation and activities offered. First a few of the ladies started comparing their various recipes for preserves and pies, which quickly turned into a competition judged by the menfolk. Someone set up a contest to see whose mules could plow a furrow the quickest and straightest. And there were nightly card games. Someone pulled out a fiddle, and someone else joined in with a banjo, and then the dancing started. Before they knew it, they'd created an organized, annual week-long community festival.

Jim finished explaining all of this as they pulled into the fairgrounds, the likes of which Cam and Tad had never seen before. Tad was wide-eyed and speechless as they drove past the rows of brightly colored cottages that formed the four sides of an acres-wide square, looking for all the world like an oversized construction of children's toy blocks. Aside from the rainbow of colors, all the cottages were roughly the same in size and design, built close together and sometimes sharing a wall. Some were even three stories high. At the very center of the open square was the main pavilion, a roofed, raised structure painted white, with a bannistered railing encircling it. A number of smaller structures edged the outside of the main clearing, serving as booths for offering all manner of treats or games of chance. On this, the first day of The Fair, things were just beginning to bustle. Families were moving into their temporary quarters, the fancy bunting was going up around the main pavilion, and displays of prized watermelons, tomatoes, and preserves were being lovingly arranged.

The Mannings' cottage was two levels, painted bright red, and sported a sign with their name on it, hand-carved and gilded. It was situated in the middle of the western side of the square, and their ample back porch had an excellent view of the racetrack behind them. The single room on the first floor contained a small cooking area, a table with chairs, and four cots where the Mannings would sleep. One was no longer needed. A steep set of stairs, more like a ladder, led to a second floor loft. Cam had to stoop slightly to keep from hitting his head on the rafters, but the space had enough room for a three-drawer chest and two bedrolls, all the space he and Tad would need for the week. Windows on front and back let the breezes through.

As they were stowing away their few belongings, Jim called from downstairs. "I'd suggest that you boys get on over to the stables and register for the harness-racing."

"Ya mean to say we can run them horses, too?" Tad's face lit up with an excited grin. "They'll let us do that our own selves, Massah James?"

"Why, sure they will, if you've a mind to."

Tad spun toward Cam. "Hey, you wanna, Camel? Ya wanna we should race them horses in that buggy race?"

"Yeah, I can't see why not..." Campbell hesitated, recalling Tad's attempts at controlling Ol' Prince, the mule. But they were here to have fun and try new things, so he relented. "As long as you think you can keep the buggy on the track," he teased.

"Ain't no need you worryin' y'sef 'bout that, Camel. As long as they gives me a real horse instead of that mule to pull my buggy, I's gonna win that race." Tad was already down the ladder and running out the door. "Well, c'mon, Camel, let's us get on over there and get lined up for them races before you decides better!"

As Campbell hurried to catch up to Tad, he called back over this shoulder, "Care to join us, Jim?"

Jim had already settled into a rocker on the porch. "I'll just wait and watch you fellas do a couple of laps... sorta feel out my competition."

At the northern end of the track, there was a hand-lettered sign tacked up on the paddock fence that announced "Harness Racing—sign up here". After paying their entrance fee and getting assignments as to horse and heat number, Cam and Tad studied the little herd of fillies and geldings that would pull the racing buggies.

Climbing up to stand on the bottom rail of the fence, Tad pointed to a big chestnut with a white hour-glass blaze. "That's mine, right there."

"How do you know that?"

"Cuz he's got lots of muscles and that there big ol' chest. He can run."

"I think you'll get whichever one is..." Cam checked the tickets. "...Henrietta."

"I ain't gonna race no horse called Henrietta." Tad sneered the name.

Cam chuckled. "Why don't we go get something to eat. I hear the band starting up over at the pavilion."

The stand selling roasted ears of corn had just opened up, and the ones they bought were fresh, sweet and hot. They ambled between the cottages over to the pavilion and sat side by side on the soft, green lawn, munching their corn, dripping butter down their arms, and listened to the brass band warm up with a couple of slow tunes. When they got into the marches, Tad couldn't contain himself, jumping up to prance and wiggle to the spirited beat.

As lively as it was, the music only aroused a deep melancholy in Cam. This time the memory didn't come at him like a bolt of lightening, but more like a wave of deep, cold water pulling him down into a dark place. He'd marched away to war, away from Mary Frances, away from everything he loved, to that martial beat. He could feel the heat of the blindingly bright day, when all the young men from around Jackson County had dressed in their crisp new uniforms and been hailed as heroes, heralded off to defend the South with the brass band playing "Dixie". But it was a vague, incomplete image, as if he were straining to look up at it through the deep water.

It drained away as quickly as it had washed over him. He shook his head and stood, taking the still-frolicking Tad by the shoulders. "Let's go and watch a couple of races. That way maybe we can look more like we know what we're doing by the time our heat comes up."

This is going to be interesting, Cam thought, as he watched the various versions of small, one-seated buggies, each pulled by a single horse, whiz around the half-mile track. There was nothing standardized about the home-made carts, and certainly nothing standard about the variety of horses. Evidently there were some who brought their own horse and cart just for this competition, but most were like Cam and Tad, who laid down their entry fee and took their chances.

After watching three different races, it was their turn, and Tad rushed ahead of him toward the stables. When Cam got there, Tad was already mounted on the seat of his buggy, reins in hand. Henrietta, despite her name, looked like a sturdy, capable animal. His own dappled gelding was a little long in the tooth, but with some skill, Cam thought he might have a chance at least to finish the race. It was all for fun, anyway, and Tad was certainly bursting with the thrill of it.

Jostling for position with the three other competitors, they pulled up to the starting line. When the starter fired his pistol, all five horses leapt forward in a dead heat.

Tad had pulled ahead of him, setting a good pace, but half way around the track, Henrietta lost interest in the pursuit and slowed to a gentle trot. Then she decided she was hungry and turned to head back to her stall. Tad was shouting a blue streak and pulling on the reins, but it was a losing battle.

While trying to keep an eye on Tad, Cam lost control of his own horse, who was still racing, but not necessarily in a straight line. He reined the horse in just in time for Tad's Henrietta nearly to collide with the back of his buggy.

By the time Cam and Tad had finished a complete circuit of the track, the winner was already being announced. However, the spectators were graceful enough to give them a hearty round of applause for at least finishing the course still mounted on their buggies.

A brilliant orange sun had finally disappeared behind the stables on the far side of the race track, leaving behind its fading, streaked afterglow on the darkening sky, and the sounds of the evening were just beginning. The crickets and cicadas were warming up, not to be outdone by the music drifting from the main pavilion. The porch's floor boards creaked rhythmically in time to Jim's rocking chair, and the chains suspending the swing from the porch ceiling added a counter note as Mamie and Sudie gently glided back and forth in small arcs.

Cam sat quiet and still in his own rocking chair and absently watched Tad sitting on the steps at his feet, leaning against the porch railing and whittling on a stick with the small knife Jim had given him. The conversation swirled around the buggy race, and the baking competition, and plans for the next day, but Cam's thoughts were where they always seemed to end up lately. He tried to imagine that moment when he would reveal his dark secret to the Mannings, but when he got to the part where he pictured their reaction, his mind recoiled from it, as if stung by a bee.

"I wonder what kind of wiles a young lady would have to use to entice a fine gentleman of quality to escort her on a moonlight stroll?"

Cam looked up to see Sudie Anne standing by his chair.

"Why, my brazen daughter... " Mamie gently chastised.

"Hey, that's a good iddy!" Tad tossed his stick into the yard and jumped up. "Let's us take Miss Sudie for a nice walk."

Campbell quickly regrouped his thoughts. "Let's Camel take Miss Sudie for a nice walk, and let's Tademus take himself on up to bed. That way, maybe by the time I crawl into mine, I won't be required to do any more gabbing for one day, excepting for my nightly prayers. How's that for a 'good iddy'?"

"Oh, I gets it," Tad grinned. "Ya'll is just wantin' to get away for a little spoonin', ain't ya?"

"What you're aiming to get is a little 'tanning', young man. Now, on up to bed with you and don't forget to say your prayers."

"Yessah, Camel." Tad sighed heavily, but accepted his fate and started inside, stopping in the doorway. "Goodnight Massah Jim, Miz Mannin'."

"Goodnight, Tademus," Mamie smiled.

Jim added, "You sleep well, young man."

With a big grin and a wink, Tad turned back one last time, coyly mocking, "'Nite, Miss Sudie...."

"Tademus Co..." Cam threatened. Tad quickly disappeared into the cabin, letting the screen door slam behind him.

Cam pushed out of the rocker, extending his arm to Sudie Anne. "Shall we? Before Tademus decides on a return engagement?"

At the end of the row of cottages, a gravel path led out beyond the racetrack and down by the river, where a nearly-full moon lighted their way. They strolled in companionable silence for a long time, Cam acutely aware of Sudie's warm hand on his arm. Just one of the many small blessings he'd come to treasure that now he was destined to lose.

Pulling gently on his arm, Sudie lead him to one of the wooden benches that adorned along the path, and they sat close together, looking out over the moon-shimmering water. Back up the river, the distant sparkling lights of the pavilion blended with the sky, looking like mischievous stars that had escaped Heaven to come join in the festivities. Strains of music drifted to them on the fragrant breeze, too faint to make out a tune.

Sudie Anne finally broke the silence. "He loves you, you know. He loves you very much."

"He's a good boy. I hope he has a good life ahead of him."

"How'd the two of you come to be..." Sudie Anne searched for the right word. "...to be so close?"

"Oh, our lives just sort of came together, I guess."

"Has any of that time...that time, I mean, before your accident...begun to come back to you?"

Cam leaned forward, away from her, and rested his elbows on his knees. It almost escaped from his mouth, almost leaped out before he could stop it. He needed so badly to unburden himself. But not here, and not now, on this perfect, soft evening. "This is a mighty heavy bit of talking we're getting into on such a beautiful night as this, don't you think?" he said instead.

"Yes, you're right. It is a lovely night, at that."

"And what about Miss Sudie? How come she hasn't graced any of those suitors who're bound to have been coming around courting? There must be somebody she's been inclined to favor with her attentions?"

"Well, there was before things began to happen."

"Things?"

"You know, before we got the news..." Sudie dropped her eyes and fiddled with her sleeve. "There was a friend of Marler's..."

It was almost as if the dark specter of her brother wouldn't be denied. Cam needed to change the subject before he weakened. "That's some happy-sounding fiddling coming from the pavilion. Care to show me a few steps?"

"That's an inspiring idea," she agreed, the lightness returning to her voice. "Or 'iddy', as Master Tademus would say."

Cam started to take Sudie's arm to escort her on to the 'ball', but she stopped short, placing her hand on his elbow. "Campbell..." She held his eyes for a long moment. "I hope you stay."

She wouldn't be saying that if she knew the truth, Campbell thought. But he just patted her hand, and they strolled away toward the music.

One dance had just ended, and the musicians were tuning up for the next, as the crowd of dancers rearranged themselves on the pavilion dance floor. Taking his hand, Sudie led Cam to a small knot of dancers, a couple of whom he recognized as her friends from neighboring farms. He only had a chance to nod a greeting before another lively fiddle tune began, the caller joined in, and they were all swirling around the dance floor trying to keep up with the rapid-fire "do-sa-does" and "promenades". The bright-colored lanterns flashed a dizzying rainbow over the crowd as the dance got faster and faster, partners separating, coming together, swinging and changing direction. By the time the music came to a rousing conclusion, leaving the dancers panting, laughing and applauding, Cam was just a little light-headed. He looked around for Sudie, who had been promenaded off by another young man at some point in the action. But he didn't see her.

Still hanging on his arm was the partner he'd ended the dance with, a petite, bright-eyed brunette in pink gingham with a matching bow in her long hair.

She dipped her head and looked up at him through thick lashes. "Why, my, my, I do believe that this old fair is just beginning to attract all kinds of newcomers to its midst." Slightly breathless, either from the dance or by design, she extended one delicate gloved hand. "I'm Faye Prisk. But you can call me Faye Prissy. Near 'bout everybody does."

Cam took the offered hand and raised it to his lips for the obligatory kiss. "I imagine they do."

"What does everybody call you?"

"Campbell." He searched over the heads of the departing crowd, again trying to catch a glimpse of Sudie's bright blonde hair.

Miss Prissy moved in closer. "Why, you look absolutely lost, Stranger Camel."

"Campbell," he corrected, bristling at her use of Tad's special name for him. "It's Campbell, with a 'bell'."

"Well, there's no call for you to go and get all huffy about it, Campbell-with-a-bell... ding, ding." She pantomimed ringing a tiny bell with one hand as she wrapped the other snuggly back around Campbell's arm. "Why doesn't little Ole Faye just give Mr. Campbell-with-a-bell a grand tour of our fair fair-grounds?" She giggled at her own play on words.

From the distinct aroma of bourbon mingled with the fragrance of rose water with which she'd abundantly splashed herself, it was obvious that much of this hospitality Miss Prissy was displaying, she had swallowed from a bottle. "Better than that," Cam suggested, "why don't I help you look for the beau you came in with?"

"Chances are, I might just've found myself a brand new one." Her arm tightening around his, she leaned against him and raised a lace hanky to her painted red lips. "My, I do believe I'm getting the vapors," she moaned, in no threat to any leading lady John Wilkes Booth may have played opposite.

People were staring at them, some questioningly, others smiling knowingly. He needed to move out of this center of attention. Her waist was so slender that his arm fit almost all the way around her as he supported her toward the steps leading down off the dance floor and toward the lemonade stand. A certain relief flooded through him when he found Sudie already there, in the middle of a gathering of young folk, sipping from a tall, frosty glass.

"Oh, I was wondering how you got sidetracked, Campbell," Sudie called out as Cam and his new friend approached. Quickly assessing his predicament, Sudie added, with the barest twinkle in her eyes, "But I can see now how you got derailed."

The rest of the group turned to face him.

Abruptly his focus narrowed onto one face. The ground shifted beneath his feet, and the rest of the world vanished, replaced by a wet beach, a hot morning, the smell of blood, death and gunpowder. The man's name was Lucas. He'd held a rifle pointed at Cam's chest, declaring that he was going to get him one last Reb before the war was over.

Recognition flashed in the face of the man named Lucas, and his smile dissolved into pure hatred. "Yeah, I've been wondering what became of you, too...Campbell."

Sudie's head swiveled back and forth between the two of them. "You mean you two know each other?"

"Oh, I know him, Sudie Anne." Lucas' eyes burned so intensely that Campbell could almost feel the heat. "He knows me, too, and what's more interesting than all that, he knew your brother."

"Marler? You mean you think that Cam, here, knew Marler?" Sudie shook her head resolutely. "No, you're mistaken, Lucas! You must be confused!"

Lucas calmly poured the remainder of his lemonade into the dirt and thumped his glass onto the counter. "Yes, it is confusing, isn't it, Sudie? But it's even more bizarre than you could ever possibly imagine."

Campbell knew it was coming. It was a nightmare from which he couldn't awaken, that had him standing there on the tracks, unable to move a muscle in the path of an on-coming locomotive.

"Campbell, here," Lucas declared, finally breaking eye contact with Cam and looking around him for support from his cronies. "Cam, here, is the man who killed Marler. Woulda killed me, too, if I hadn't managed to get away."

Lucas turned to face Sudie Anne and growled again, "He killed your brother, Sudie Anne."

Sudie took a step back, the color draining from her face. "No, that can't be right. Tell him, Campbell, he's mistaken..." This was incredulous.

Lucas swung on Campbell again. "This man's a friend of yours? And you don't even know that he murdered your own brother in cold blood? That is bizarre, now, wouldn't you agree, Reb?"

This was not the way it was suppose to happen. In his worst imaginings, this was never the way it would turn out. Cam felt Sudie move away from him as if he were contaminated and abhorrent, heard her gasp and begin to sob.

It ripped his heart open, and a raging demon exploded from inside. He launched himself at Lucas, plunging through the lemonade stand, sending wood and glass flying. They hit the ground hard, and when his fists started slamming into flesh, they wouldn't stop. Again and again his fists smashed into the sneering ugly face...

A crowd of men was suddenly on top of him. He struggled to pull from a tight grip on his arm and the strangle-hold around his neck, and he landed two more solid punches before they could pin him to the ground, as he gasped for breath. Slowly the demon withered and died, leaving him hollow and exhausted, Sudie's sobbing echoing inside his head as her friends led her away.

Campbell was arrested for assault and taken to the Jefferson City Jail that same night. The next morning another charge was added—that of first degree murder of one Marler Stone Manning.

ACCOUNTABILITY

photography by BB

CHAPTER
22

THAT NIGHT AT THE FAIR had been just as chaotic and frightening as the night the Massah's plantation had gone up in flames. It was like the world was on fire, out of control, and no one knew what to do. Miz Sudie, breathless and practically hysterical, had dragged Tad from his bedroll and told him to get dressed. They were leaving. Massah Jim was laying Miz Manning out in the back of the buckboard and covering her with a quilt. At first Tad had thought she was dead. When he'd asked where Camel was, no one would answer him, or even look at him. All Sudie had said was, "Get in the wagon, Tademus. I'll explain later." As scared as he'd been, he'd come to love and trust these people, so he'd done as he was told, gripping the wagon seat tightly as Miz Sudie drove the little mare into a fast canter over the rutted road to home.

After Miz Sudie had sat him down at the kitchen table and told him what had happened, he still didn't believe it. Somebody was not tellin' him right, or had gotten the facts mixed up, or was just plain crazy. Camel never killed anybody, except when he had a good reason to, like in the war.

As one day ended and the next began, Tad went about his routine, feeding and watering the livestock, collecting the eggs, mucking out the barn. Sudie would fix his meals, but she rarely spoke anymore, and never smiled. Miz Manning had barely woken up, and when she did, all she could do was cry. Massah Jim never left her room, and Dr. Lester came out to the farm every day. It was like Tad was a shadow. No one took much notice of him.

Late on Wednesday afternoon, Tad sneaked in the back door as quietly as the rusty hinges allowed, and set on the kitchen table the basket of wildflowers he'd picked. As usual, he was afraid any noise would somehow intrude on the solemn despair that had fallen over the household. He'd thought the brightly colored flowers would bring some much needed cheer, but now the blooms, beginning to wilt in the basket, looked sadly inadequate.

While milking the goats that morning, he'd finally worked up the nerve to ask if he could go into town and visit Camel in jail. If they said no, he was going to do it anyway. Camel needed him, and was probably thinking he'd abandoned him. From the back bedroom, he could hear the voices of Massah Jim and Dr. Lester. He pulled out one of the kitchen chairs, careful not to let it scrape the floor, and sat down, straining to listen.

"Jim, I want to be as tactful as I know how in what I'm about to say."

"Please, just say it, Doc." Massah Jim sounded scared and very tired.

"Well, I think we would be wise in taking precautions against the possibility of... well, of Miz Mamie's bringing some harm to herself."

"You mean of her trying to claim her own life?"

Dr. Lester cleared this throat. "She's in a state of extreme, deep depression, and I just..."

"Doctor." Massah Jim cut him off. "Our faith... its foundation would never support such a theory as you're suggesting"

"Jim, I'm not expecting you to condone this theory. I'm simply suggesting that we recognize its possibility and try to avoid its happening. Don't you understand that she could be without control over her own will, whatever it may be?"

"No!" Massah Jim's shout made Tad jump. "Don't you understand, Doctor Lester, that Mamie's God is not without control?"

"James..." It was the first time Tad had heard Miz Mamie speak since they'd gotten back from the fair, and it was so weak that he could hardly hear what she was saying.

"I'm right here, Darlin'. I'm right here by you." Massah Jim spoke softly but urgently, his voice cracking a little.

"Campbell...he never could have done this." Her words were only a hoarse whisper, but Tad's heart leapt. At least there was someone else who believed the way he did.

Even from his jail cell, Campbell had heard the news and gossip from around town. Deputy Jones was always eager to share with him what everyone was saying about the most sensational news since the war ended, or to show him the newspaper articles and editorials. It seemed that everyone's mind was made up, and the verdict was already loudly and clearly being proclaimed all over town: Davis Campbell McCool was guilty of the willful murder in the first degree of beloved local hero, Marler Stone Manning. And execution by hanging would certainly be the sentence.

As Campbell lay on the hard bunk during those hot, sleepless nights, and paced the cell and stared at the blank stone walls as the day's sun crawled across the floor, he prayed constantly for forgiveness for what he knew were his real crimes—that he had ingratiated himself into the Manning family without having made any effort to disclose the truth concerning his part in Marler's death. Then he had virtually taken the boy's place with the parents, and positioned himself to his own advantage with the Mannings' daughter.

These were all the extra nails the court of public opinion would hand to the jury to hammer into his coffin.

It was just after nightfall on Wednesday when Tad was led into the cell block carrying Campbell's supper. Cam bounced off his cot, thrilled to see the boy still clean and healthy, if not smiling. He'd been told that the Mannings were caring for him but had still worried. "Well, if it ain't ol' Tademus Co of Marion County, Mis'sippi!" Cam tried to keep his tone lighter than his heart felt.

Tad carefully carried the supper tray over to Cam's cell and slid it under the door. "Camel, there's plenty bad talkin' goin' around. It don't look too good for us."

"You can't believe everything you hear, you know." Cam wondered if his smile looked as forced as it felt.

Tad didn't fall for it. "Talk has you killin' Massah James and Miz Mamie's boy in cold blood... after the war was done already over with. It wa'n't that way. It wa'n't like that at all, were it Camel?" Tad clung to the cell bars as if he could climb through them. "I just knows it ain't true! I knows you didn't kill nobody like folks is sayin'!"

Campbell looked into the wide, dark eyes of his 10-year-old ward, suddenly realizing that telling the Mannings the truth was actually not the hardest part. "I did kill him, Tademus." When the boy's shoulders slumped and tears welled up, Cam quickly clarified. "It wasn't like folks are saying it was, though. It was an accident. I didn't intend for it to happen."

"It was sorta like with me and my Pa, maybe huh, wa'n't it Camel?" Tad winced slightly at the memory. "You know... maybe 'se'f defense'?"

"Listen to me, Tad." Campbell stooped down to face the boy eye to eye. "I want you to put all those thoughts about your Pa's accident out of your head, do you hear me? That's all behind you. Do you understand what I'm saying?"

"Yeah, but you said it y'sef. You just said it was an accident with my Pa, just like it was with you and the Manning boy, Mistah Marler."

"You're right. They were both accidents."

"Well, if they's just alike, your accident and mine, then they's bound to set you free, ain't they, just like they done with me?"

Squeezing his eyes shut before his own tears escaped, Cam desperately searched for the words to explain the inconsistencies of the criminal justice system to a slave boy who'd always thought white people got all the justice. He finally gave up. "They're just not the same, Tademus. We'll have to wait and see, son. We'll just have to wait."

As they'd played a half-hearted game of checkers through the bars, Cam tried to choke down the tasteless mush and stale bread Tad had brought him. The meal could have been steak with all the trimmings, and Cam knew it would have tasted the same. When Tad started yawning, Cam convinced him to return to the farm and get a good night's sleep. Tad left only after vowing that he'd be back the next day, after his chores were done.

Cam had settled back onto the cot and drifted into an uneasy doze when he heard the cell block door swinging open again. He raised his head, thinking it was Deputy Jones coming for his dinner dishes. "You're popular tonight, McCool," the Deputy drawled. "Got another visitor."

From behind Jones, Jim moved into the light of the oil lamp and walked toward the cell. Cam crossed over to meet him at the bars.

He'd not seen Jim since that night at the fair. Dark circles rimmed his eyes and his sparse white hair was uncombed. For long minutes, he stared into Cam's eyes, burning a hole to his very soul. Finally, Jim spoke quietly and directly. "I've but one question to put to you, to which there are but two possible answers, either requiring but one word. I want to hear the truthful one. Did you kill my son?"

Campbell drew in a deep breath. He'd been aching to say this for so long. Why was it now so hard? "Jim, I. . ."

"That's two words, " Jim interrupted, "and no answer."

Cam fought the immediate urge to look at the floor, the ceiling, the walls—anywhere but into Jim's red-rimmed eyes. But he had to face his deeds and this man squarely. "Yes."

A frown crumpled Jim's weathered face, aging him beyond his years. But it was not the hate Cam had expected to see. Instead it was a deep, bottomless grief.

"'Vengeance is mine, sayeth the Lord. . .' May He show mercy upon your soul." Jim turned from Campbell and exited the cellblock.

DUST TO DUST

CHAPTER
23

IS CELL WAS TURNING from black to grey with the early morning light, but Cam had been awake for hours. When he was able to sleep, it was only in short, troubled naps that left him more agitated than rested. This night had been no different, his dreams filled with shadowy dangers he couldn't seem to escape.

This was the quietest time of the morning, before the town began to come alive with the business of the day. No wagons rattled up the cobbled street, no merchants called out to customers from shop doorways. Even the jailhouse was silent, there being no other prisoners at the moment, and its being too early for the night jailer to turn his shift over to Deputy Jones. Breakfast was still a couple of hours away.

A sharp noise, like a chair falling over, snapped him alert. He leaned up on one elbow, trying to determine where the sound had come from, and holding his breath, listening for another. Only silence rang in his ears. Maybe it was a rat. Or maybe he imagined it. He was about to lie back down when the hinges creaked on the outer cell block door down the hall. Maybe Deputy Jones was serving breakfast early this morning. Cam had never given Jones credit for that much initiative.

But the passageway remained dark. The oil lamp didn't flare into light. As Cam swiveled to his feet, all he could see was the bulky shadow of the night jailer easing slowly through the door and toward his cell. As the shadow drew closer, he saw there was a smaller one following the first. Tademus, looking unsubstantial next to the beefy guard, held a shot-gun with its muzzle pressed against the guard's neck, just under his right ear.

"Oh God, no, Tad...no..." Please let this be a lingering nightmare, Cam prayed. He'd been telling himself things couldn't get any worse, and now they suddenly had. The firing pins to both barrels of the scatter-gun were cocked, and the jailer's wide-eyed expression made it clear he realized even the slightest sudden movement could leave him with a head full of buckshot.

"Throw him the keys." Tad gave the gun a jerk for emphasis, making the substantial folds of the guards neck jiggle like jelly.

"Tad, please don't do this..."

"I's already doing it, Camel." Again he pushed the gun against the guard's neck.

As carefully as possible, the jailer reached into a deep pocket, pulled out the heavy ring of keys, and tossed them toward Cam's cell. They hit the bars with a reverberating clang, and fell to the floor at his feet.

"C'mon, Camel, hurry it up, get your cell opened. I's got four horses tied up outside."

"You stole horses?" Could this get any worse?

"C'mon, we's gotta get movin'!"

It was too late now to do anything but let the nightmare play out. Cam scooped up the keys, separated out the long one that fit his cell, and reaching through the bars awkwardly, managed to get the door open. The first thing he did was ease the shotgun out of Tad's hands.

"Into the cell." Cam backed up the order by nudging the guard on the arm with the gun's barrel. The guard obeyed wordlessly, and Campbell pushed the barred door closed behind him. "If there is so much as a belch or a fart from you, there's gonna be hair and blood all over this cell. Got it?"

The guard nodded his understanding and sat heavily on the cot.

As they quickly made their way down the passageway to the rear door, the reality hit him like a physical jolt. They were committed beyond redemption now. No matter how explainable the accident of Marler Manning's death might be, he and Tad were now true criminals, and there was no turning back.

"Did you see anybody around about, stirring in the streets, when you came in?" Cam whispered before opening the back door.

"Nothin' exceptin' ol' man Luther Lamar sweepin' out his saloon for the early risers. And him still so gut-full his own se'f from last night he weren't even hardly able to keep his feet under him."

"Nobody else?"

Tad shook his head.

Campbell twisted the doorknob gently, and the door swung outward on rusty hinges. He and Tad stepped out into the early morning light of the empty alley. "Tad, where'd you leave the horses?"

Tad's head swiveled in all directions. His voice echoed out into the street. "Right over yonder, Camel, I swears. I done tied them up right over there by that old water trough!"

"Suussshh!" If anyone heard them, this crazy stunt was over before it even got started. "Well, they must've gotten loose, somehow."

"I tied them up, Camel! I tied them up real good, what with the two we'd pull behind us already hitched up to the two we'd ride and everything."

The sun was just beginning to rise above the court-house roof, sparking in bright streaks down the main street.

This was the pivotal moment. They either left now and got far away before anyone discovered they were gone, or they stayed to face their fate, whatever it might be. He looked down at the scared, brave little boy huddled next to him, who'd risked everything to do what he felt was right. Campbell made a decision. Whether it were the right decision or not, it didn't seem to matter anymore.

"Now, listen to me, Tad, and listen carefully. I want you to stay right here. Don't wander off anywhere, no matter what, for any reason. Do you understand me? I mean it...you stay right here. Okay?"

"Okay, I will Camel...but where you off to?"

"I'm going to find our mounts...or some others just like 'em, if I can. I'll willingly settle for just two of them if I can find any at all." Cam gave Tad a reassuring pat on the shoulder and headed around the corner of the jail house into the main street.

There were lights glowing from a few of the shop windows as the merchants were starting about their business. The only other sign of life was down a block and a half in front of the Knickerbocker Hotel, Saloon and Tonsorial Parlor, where Tademus had reported seeing Luther Lamar. What he sought was tied to the hitching rail at the front of the hotel—two sturdy-looking horses fully saddled and enjoying a drink from the water trough. A brief thought as to what the penalty for horse thieving was in Missouri flashed through his head, but there was no time for worrying about those details right now.

As soon as Campbell had taken a few paces out toward the middle of the street, he heard the shout from behind him. "Just hold it right there, Reb! And no need you turning around, neither. You can just let that gun drop, too, whilst you're at it!"

The threatening drawl came out of nowhere, just as it had on that morning a lifetime ago, in the pine barrens bordering the beach at Mobile Bay. Back then, in that other universe, he'd tried to explain to Lucas that the war was over. If it hadn't worked then, it certainly wasn't going to work now. There seemed to be all too many folks around who still chose to disregard that fact.

Campbell released the shotgun as ordered, and it timbered to the ground, just like the rifle Cam had dropped into the sand on that hot April day in Alabama.

"I believe it's your turn to talk next, ain't it Reb?" Lucas sneered. "Time for you to be saying something about us being your 'friends' or something like that. Ain't that the way we done it?"

Campbell raised his hands and turned slowly to face Lucas, who was flanked this time by three of his cronies, each holding his own rifle.

"No, Lucas. At Mobile Bay, there was only one other with you. This time there are three..."

Luther Lamar had peeked out through his open door. Curious hotel customers were edging out onto the sidewalk, a couple of second floor windows over the dry goods store creaked open. No one was coming close, but everyone was watching.

"That's cute, Reb. Yeah, that's real cute. Only I wasn't figuring to need even that one down there that other time. Matter of fact, as I recall, he actually got in my way, come to think about it. And I'm sure I don't need no three here now to settle up our score."

"Why don't you just let it rest, Lucas? It's all finished. Can't you understand that?"

"Well, now Reb, that's more like it. Yeah, that there sounds more like the words I remember you saying before.

Something about 'it's all over' or something like that. Well, I'm just bound to have to keep saying it again and again to you, too, now, ain't I? Can't you understand? It ain't all over, and it ain't gonna be all over neither. Not till I get my last Reb! And this time I'm aiming to get him without no Manning comin' 'twixt us!"

Lucas unholstered his long, black Colt .44 and lifted the weapon into careful and steady aim at the center of Cam's chest for the execution.

"I'm unarmed, Lucas..."

With dramatic flare, he thumbed back the firing pin into cocked position, the clicking sound reverberating throughout the graveyard-quiet streets.

The deafening report of a single shot echoed off the buildings.

Campbell jumped, startled.

Lucas slumped, dead.

The boy stood there in his tracks for a brief moment, already dead from the bullet to his brain; then he simply gave the appearance of dropping down into a more comfortable position on his knees, with his arms falling loosely to his side and his head tilting forward, limp and bowed.

To Campbell, it looked like Lucas was praying. Finally, the body collapsed forward, face into the dust. A faint, humble cloud of powder-fine dust rose around the corpse, then drifted away on the gentle morning breeze.

"Tademus..." Campbell searched anxiously about the street and its gathering crowd. From the alleyway, moving into the brilliant spreading sunshine, stepped Jim Manning, the gun in his hand, now hanging at his side, still smoking.

As Jim walked out into the middle of the street toward Campbell, Tad simultaneously sprinted out from behind the jail. By the time Jim stood facing Cam, Tademus was throwing his arms around Cam's waist. Cam hugged the skinny little boy against him, feeling his shoulders shake with silent sobs.

He looked over Tad's head at the tall, proud man standing in front of him. "Jim... I'm sorry... I never meant to... "

"I know, son." Jim lowered his head and swallowed hard. "Come on back home, Campbell. We all want you to come back home. It's where you belong. You and the boy both, you belong with us... with the family."

REDEMPTION

photography by BB

CHAPTER

24

OVER DECADES OF CULTIVATING these fields, several
generations of Manning farmers had moved tons
of fieldstone out of the paths of their plows. Much
of it was used to build walls and smokehouses and homes
with the color and character of the land. And still there
was a wide, low cairn of stones at the edge of the eastern
pasture—some the size of a watermelon, some as big as
an outhouse—waiting patiently to be put to a good use. At
the outer edge of that pile, Campbell had found the perfect
palette for his work, almost as if God had shaped it just for
him, for this purpose—a two-foot-high piece of sandstone
with one smooth side streaked in pale pinks and blue-grays,
like a sunset. With Jim and Tad's help, he was able to pry it
from the rich soil and lever it into the hand cart, and they'd
wheeled it across the field, through the orchard, and over to
the waiting spot in the family cemetery.

Jim and Mamie had told him that it wasn't necessary, that
they'd order a memorial stone for Marler from the stone-
mason in town. But Campbell's conscience wouldn't leave
the idea alone. As everyone else had been reading or sewing
around the fireplace in the evenings, he'd borrowed Tad's
slate and chalk and, with many false starts, erasing, and revis-
ing, had drawn out the simple design that he felt in his heart.

✝

In Loving Memory
MARLER STONE MANNING
Feb. 26, 1843 - Apr. 12, 1865

When he knew it was right, he transferred the design onto the chosen stone with chalk, then started to work with hammer and chisel. It had taken him three days of slow, precise work, sitting cross-legged in front of the stone at its chosen spot in front of Marler's grandfather's grave. Now it was done. Campbell wiped away dust and stone chips with a damp rag, and leaned back from his narrow view of the final G in Manning, to take in the whole, complete carving. It wasn't professional. He could never sell his work. The F was a bit lopsided, and his chisel had taken out unnecessary nicks here and there. But his heart declared it good.

His focus had been so narrow for so long that he hadn't noticed it had begun to rain. He closed his eyes and turned his face to the leaden sky, letting the light drops fall on his face like tiny kisses. The day was warm for mid-September, but the air was changing with the rain, and as his shirt slowly dampened, a breath of a breeze sent a chill through him. He should gather his tools and go inside, but he didn't want to leave Marler again, not yet.

This little family plot was about the size of the one on his own family's land. His was surrounded by a low wrought-iron fence. This one was protected by a wall of the fieldstone that the earth in these parts so generously donated. But the meaning was the same. Family. Generations. Carrying on, one after the other, each building something better and more beautiful for the ones that follow.

His eyes came to rest on the rounded granite stone that marked the grave of Mathias Manning, Jim's father and Marler's grandfather. A simple cross was carved into the top, above the name and dates, and his Revolutionary War regiment. He'd died before Marler was born. The land had passed from one of Missouri's earliest settlers down to his son, and now the legacy ended. The beauty, that something better that had been planted and nurtured for so long, had nowhere else to go.

The end of a legacy. A promise unfulfilled. The unfathomable, unbearable death of a son. An heir. A gift from God. The awful sudden power of the memory punched the breath from his lungs as if he'd been physically assaulted. He collapsed back into the grass, dizzy and disoriented. The words on the thin, precious piece of paper swam before him in a blur just as they'd done on the night he'd first read them, before he'd committed them to memory. His father's letter had said that Mary Frances and baby Davis had been strolling the hospital grounds and had somehow ended up in the pond, drowned. Maybe Davis had wandered in first, innocently chasing a butterfly, and maybe Mary Frances had rushed after him, to pull him from beneath the lily pad-clogged waters. By the time the nurses had found them...

When the courier had delivered the letter to him at the encampment, he'd waited with barely contained excitement before he opened it, until he'd finished his rounds with his patients, and was truly free to savor the news from home. He'd settled next to the cook fire to read. He'd read it three times before the truth of it broke through to his consciousness. Then he'd sat by the fire, neither eating nor drinking, letting his orderlies attend to the wounded, for three days, buried as deeply in his darkened world as his wife and child were buried beneath the earth. He marveled that the sinuses could continue to produce so much water.

Now the tears flowed again, streaming quietly down his cheeks into the grass, and mingling with the gentle rain. His beloved wife and his precious child were dead. He'd known that. His concussion had hidden it from him for a while, but it was an old wound, thick and scabbed, that still had the power to stop his heart.

"Camel?"

Campbell blinked away the tears, wiped his face with a damp sleeve, and sat up as Tad dropped down next to him on the grass.

"That look real nice, Camel. Want I should go get the Mannings so they can have a look-see?"

"In a minute..." He put his arm around the boy and pulled him tightly against him. Tad used to be a skeleton, all skinny arms and legs, but over the last couple of months, with the help of Mamie's sumptuous meals, he'd put on some weight and developed some muscles. He'd probably grown an inch or two, as well. "Did I ever tell you that I had a family once?"

Tad pulled away from him, partly out of annoyance at being hugged, and partly to look him in the face. "I knows your Pa was a preacherman, and you was born in a cemetery whilst he learnt to be a gravedigger."

Cam laughed in spite of the dark clouds swirling over him. Tad had a way of doing that to him. For a ten-year-old, the boy had a gentle heart and an old soul. "A long time ago I had a wife, the one woman I thought God had meant just for me. And God blessed us with a son..."

Tad's voice was almost a whisper. "You never told me that. What happened?"

"God called them home to Him."

"Why'd He do that?"

The tears threatened again and choked off his words. He cleared his throat. "I wish I knew. Someday I will."

Tad seemed to mull this over for a moment as he shredded a few wet blades of grass. Finally he declared, "God is the one that brought you here, to Massah and Miz Manning, and Sudie Anne."

That's what Cam believed, but he needed to know why Tad believed it. "And why do you say that?"

"Cuz they done lost their son and needed one. So He gave them you."

"No one could ever replace Marler in their hearts. He was their flesh and blood."

"I meant a NEW son. They can still love Marler and love you, too. It's like y'all was all born into a new life, but still remembers the old one."

It was that simple. It was as if the rain had washed away a filmy layer of dust, and the clouds had parted for the bright sunshine. God didn't parcel out finite amounts of love for His children to divide among only a few. God's love was infinite, and so was man's.

"Tad, whose son are you?"

"I reckon I's the son of that ole devil Stoker Co, even if I don't wants to be."

"No, Tad, God gave you to me." Campbell pushed to his feet, and reached a hand down to pull Tad up, too. "And we have some unfinished business to take care of. You and I have to go back home, so my new son can meet my first son."

Alice shifted restlessly from one front foot to the other, feeling with a sensitivity one usually doesn't attribute to a horse, the odd mix of tension, sadness, and excitement in the air. Tad had named her after his mother, and she'd been the horse Julie Barker had hitched to the buggy the night they'd escaped from her father's twisted grasp. Alice hadn't been ridden in a while, but she was a good and dependable mount, and she'd faithfully serve Cam and Tad on the next leg of their journey. There was no brass band this time, but Cam felt the same sorrow, fear, and thrill he'd felt that spring day when he'd first marched away from his family at Mossy Point. Although they'd said their goodbyes in many different ways over the past two days, it didn't make this final parting any easier.

"Are you sure you have enough food to last you to St. Louis?" Standing at the foot of the front porch steps, Mamie hugged her shawl tightly around her shoulders and dabbed at her eyes with its fringed corner.

"Yes, ma'am. And we's gonna have enough left over to feed most everybody else on that steamboat, too," Tad assured her, hefting the bulging saddle bags up behind the saddle.

"Are you sure I can't talk you into staying, at least through the winter? You know you two are our family, right?" Jim asked one more time, holding onto the cheek piece of Alice's bridle as if it might keep her from taking them away.

Campbell gave the cinch a final tug and turned to look into the time-weathered, honest face of the man who had saved his life. "I know, Jim. We love you. Tad and I both do. We love you all. And we can never thank you enough for all that you've done for us." He looked up at Mamie, who had now been joined by Sudie Anne, holding onto her mother's arm. "But we belong together, Tad and me. We're a family, too. It just sorta seems like that's the way it's suppose to be, you know? And we have something important we need to do together. As a family."

"You will write, won't you?" Sudie Anne asked.

"And you'll come back before too long?" Mamie added.

"Of course. On both counts." Campbell shook Jim's hand,

holding onto the powerful grip for an extra moment, then he turned and hoisted himself into the saddle.

With a grave frown, meant to disguise threatening tears, Tad also stood square shouldered in front of Jim and shook his hand. "I's gonna miss you, Massah Jim." The boy's brimming eyes turned to the women. "Miz Manning. Miz Sudie..."

After each had hugged Tad again, he reached up, and Cam grabbed his arm, pulling him up behind him onto Alice's rump. With no other words left to say, Cam reined Alice eastward to begin the journey home.

STAINS WASHED AWAY
AND
FAMILY RECLAIMED

CHAPTER

25

I F THIS IS WHAT IT FELT LIKE to be a real father, Cam had begun to think that maybe the job wasn't all it was made out to be. When they'd gotten to St. Louis, Tad had not wanted to sell Alice, and he'd invented a number of vexing ways to be bullheaded about it, thoroughly testing Cam's patience.

"It's like selling my Ma," he'd moaned. Cam reminded him that the horse was not actually a reincarnation of his mother.

"She could come on the boat with us." That was not in their budget.

"But what if her new master beats her?" With that argument, the boy had a point, and they'd delayed their departure for three days until they'd found the one interested buyer in all of eastern Missouri, Tad felt, would treat Alice with the reverence she deserved.

The ride south on the Mighty Mississippi had been faster than the churning upriver trip back in the Spring. Tad had made up for all his earlier childish whining by insisting on taking up his old post as cabin boy aboard the boat. They were hiring, and his previous experience secured him the job. Cam spread his bedroll out in his favored position on an upper leeward deck, and settled in for the slow, scenic trip. Tad quickly worked his way up to head cabin boy on the same deck, with a cozy little billet he shared with two other boys. During the two week journey, Cam sorely missed having Tad at his side, and their long conversations, and nightly schooling and prayer rituals. Tad was always cheerfully busy with his duties, or instructing the newer boys. Even during his time off, he was coming up with ideas for keeping things running smoothly, trying them out, and discussing them with the head steward.

"That's one whip-smart, go-getter of a ward you got there, Mr. McCool," the steward had told him one evening, when they'd met up in the dining room. "That kind of attitude will serve him well."

Cam had grinned to himself all the way through dinner. That must be what being a father really felt like.

As Cam watched the gravedigger throw the last shovelfuls of sandy Mississippi soil onto the mounds that now marked the graves of his wife and son, he found warmth and comfort in hugging Tad closer to his side, renewing the truth that life does, indeed, go on. It doesn't just end. It continues in but one of two places. It continues with the Lord or absent from Him.

When they'd finally arrived in Mossy Point a few weeks ago, Cam had wired Dr. Bryce at the Alabama State Hospital for the Insane and arranged for the remains of Mary Frances and Davis to be returned for burial in the McCool family plot. They'd arrived by train early this morning.

Cam still had to keep reminding himself that those two wooden boxes now resting next to his parents only contained the earthly remains of two precious souls who had gone on ahead of him to the Promised Land. Mary Frances and Davis were with him now only in his memories, but one day they'd reunite in Heaven, to be together again for Eternity. That was the real truth he had to hang onto, and the reality was that Campbell DID hang onto it and DID believe it.

Tad fidgeted in his grasp. Cam realized that he might be embracing the boy a bit tightly, and loosened his hold.

"If the church ain't got no preacher since your Pa died, then who's gonna say words over these graves tomorrow?" Tad asked.

"Well, I reckon Deacon Partee won't mind doing a reading and saying a few words. He's been leading Sunday worship, and he and Mrs. Partee were quite fond of Mary Frances."

"Ain't you gonna say nothing?"

It had been on his mind. It would be only appropriate, with his father's congregation gathered for the occasion. But he hadn't been able to come up with anything to say that he could actually finish without breaking down. Just the thought of such words made his eyes well-up. But he'd think of something, and get through it somehow.

"Anything else you be needing, Dr. McCool?" the young gravedigger asked as he loaded his tools back into his wagon.

"No, thank you, Wallace." Cam pulled several coins from his pocket and handed them to the young man. "It was kind of you to do this on such short notice."

"My privilege, sir. Anything for you and your family." After stowing the coins safely in a pocket, Wallace reached into the back of his wagon and picked up a large brown envelope. "This came for you with the coffins. Sorry I forgot about it earlier. Good day to you and the boy." With that, Wallace tipped his cap and climbed onto the driver's seat, snapping the reins to head the horses out toward Hanging Moss Road.

Cam turned the slim envelope in his hands. Written in bold, neat cursive on the front was Campbell's name, and beneath that was printed: "Clinical and Observational Notes - Mary Frances McCool".

Tad peered down at the writing. "What that say, Camel?"

"Apparently it's Mary Frances' medical records. I guess Dr. Bryce thought I should have them."

"So's you'd know what good care they took of her and the baby."

"I suppose." Campbell wasn't sure this was something he wanted to read. His trained doctor's mind had already drawn for him disturbing clinical diagrams of what the coffins contained. He'd rather banish those images and remember the lively, radiant young woman who had been his wife, and the precious, innocent child who would never grow to manhood. He shook himself out of those dark places and turned to Tad. "Weren't you going to try to catch that old granddaddy catfish for our dinner?"

"Sure thing!" Tad grabbed the fishing pole that was never far from his grasp these last few weeks, and headed toward the graveyard gate. "That big ole fish ain't long for this world, so you can go ahead and grease up that skillet, Preacherman. And if'n this here pole don't do it for Mister Catfish I just bound to be diving right on into that muddy creek after him. I seen old man Jense do that and he swim around under that muddy water for more than two minutes and then come up a-holding Mister Catfish just a wiggling and Mister Jense arms all bloody."

"Well, young Ahab, you just finesse Mister What's-his-name with your pole and fishing hook. I'll have the skillet hot," Cam promised as he watched Tad trot across the meadow and down toward the creek. When he'd disappeared from sight, into the woods, Cam finally turned from the new graves and trudged back to their camp site near the remains of his boyhood home.

A parishioner had given them a surplus Army tent to use as shelter, and over the weeks, it had taken on the comfortable, lived-in aura of a home. There were always embers in the fire pit ready to be stoked for cooking or warmth, and clothes fresh from a good scrubbing in the creek hung from a line strung between two trees. Tad fished in the creek, and the two of them hunted in the surrounding countryside, in all the same spots where, as a boy, Cam had hunted deer, squirrels and dragons.

When they'd first arrived, Cam had made an inventory of what remained of the ruined homestead. His original thought had been that he'd rebuild here and make a life for himself and Tad. But he hadn't been able to make himself begin that task. A lot of ghosts still lived here, not all of them welcoming.

Cam pulled out the heavy cast-iron skillet he'd salvaged from his mother's burned kitchen and checked their supply of bacon grease, then settled himself cross-legged onto his bedroll inside the tent, out of the warm autumn sun. The envelope from Dr. Bryce sat next to him, patiently imploring him. He couldn't stare it down. His need to know won out over his desire for blissful ignorance.

Picking it up carefully, as if it would crumble, Cam studied the drab brown envelope that contained the last record on earth of his wife and son. It should be larger, more weighty, brighter and prettier. It should contain loving, colorful keepsakes, photographs, party invitations, the happy scrawlings of a toddler imagining his world. He knew it didn't.

Cam finally broke the wax seal and slipped out the thin stack of papers snugged inside. On top was a letter from Dr. Bryce on the hospital's embossed letterhead. In a bold, quick hand, the good doctor expressed his sorrow and sympathy over the untimely deaths of Mary Frances and Davis, and his hope that the enclosed material would help Campbell to understand and accept the terrible tragedy. Finding his vision going blurry, Cam quickly skimmed the following pages of hand-written notes, all describing Mary Frances' desultory state of mind, her erratic bursts of anger, despondency and continued refusal to take care of her child.

There were also notes about Davis, and how he seemed to be thriving in spite of his mother's abandonment. The nurses lovingly recorded his first steps and his first words, the favorite rag doll he slept with every night, and the time he fell and scraped a knee while chasing a duckling. Cam had to put the pages down and take a deep breath. Closing his eyes, he crossed his arms over his raised knees and rested his head on them, savoring the scenes in his mind. This was the picture he wanted to carry with him forever.

When he felt the vision tucked firmly away in a warm spot in his memory, he forced himself to resume leafing through the papers. The last were copies of the letters Dr. Bryce had written to Campbell's father, reporting on Mary Frances' condition—the information his father had then passed on to him wherever he happened to be at the time. The very last letter reported on their deaths.

Desperately he wanted to avoid reliving that night when he'd read his father's account by the camp cook fire, but some perverse compulsion forced him to focus on the page, to face it again, one last time. When he reached the middle of the page, the rest of the text dissolved into a cold fog. The only paragraph he saw read:

> "...Upon conducting evening rounds, it was discovered that Mrs. McCool and the child were not in their room. An immediate search was undertaken throughout the hospital property. It was well past midnight when she and the child were finally discovered in the shallows of the pond at the eastern edge of the property. Next to the pond, the cotton night clothes she and the child had been wearing were folded neatly and placed side by side in the precise center of a circle of candles approximately five

*feet across. Some were still lit, and
some had burned out. Next to the cloth-
ing a message had been scratched in the
dirt: 'I love you, Campbell'."*

He read it a again. And again. But he still could make no
sense of it. Folded night clothes and a ring of candles. Mary
Frances and the child wandering into the water. After careful
ritual preparation. On purpose. Not an accident. His father
had salved the truth.

The ground tilted beneath him, and Cam dropped his head
between his knees. But it didn't stop the images from swirling in his head, the same way the green algae-coated pond
water must've swirled over their heads that night, blocking
out light and air and life. He gasped for breath, momentarily
stunned that he could breathe, that he wasn't sinking into
the unfathomable depths with them. What kind of hellish
nightmare must she have been living all that time that she
felt her only escape was death, and that by taking the child
with her, in some kind of desperate hope, in the next life
their lives would be better.

He should have known what she was going through. Why
didn't he know? Was he so insensitive and consumed by
his own passion for war that he'd overlooked it somehow?
Abandoned her, the love of his life, the better half of his soul,
at a time when she needed him most? Why didn't she tell him?

Why didn't his father tell him?

In spite of his rapid panting, he was suffocating. He leapt
to his feet and bolted out through the tent flaps, desperate
for fresh air, different air. But the black truth pursued him,
even out into this sunny, late autumn afternoon.

"Hey, Camel!"

At the shout, Cam's world snapped back into focus. Tad
was running barefoot up the lane, kicking up little clouds of

dust, and waving a huge fish over his head. "We gonna eat like kings tonight!"

As Tad approached, brandishing the dead catfish, he must've sensed the dark cloud that had descended. He slowed, now dragging the fish on the ground, and approached Cam cautiously, as if he were a stranger. "What's the matter, Camel? You looks like you done seen a ghost."

Campbell opened his mouth to speak, but no words came out. He didn't have any words to put around this awful revelation that would make it endurable, explainable, or even comprehensible.

He had to hold onto something real. Something substantial and unchanging. Campbell reached out and pulled Tad to him, wrapping both arms tightly around the boy, then he slumped into the grass next to the fire pit, pulling Tad down with him. Not questioning, not squirming, Tad folded up against him. And there they stayed, Cam holding fast to his other son, until God saw fit to give him the dawn of a new day.

"... *Fear thou not; for I am with thee: be not dismayed; for I am thy God: I will strengthen thee; yea, I will help thee; yea, I will uphold thee with the right hand of my righteousness.*"

Although Cam had not slept the night before, he stood in the late morning sunshine, listening to Deacon Partee recite the quiet words of Isaiah, and felt the weariness drain from his body as if someone had pulled a plug. Sometime during the darkest hours, Cam had told Tad about what he'd learned from Dr. Bryce's notes. Speaking it aloud had made it hard and tangible, something he could twist and turn and examine from all angles, and finally put in its proper place. Now, in the crystal clarity of God's new day, he'd reached that place of peace and strength of which Isaiah spoke.

"Let us now bow our heads in prayer," Deacon Partee intoned to begin The Lord's Prayer.

Standing in front of Cam, Tad reverently lowered his head—the head that now, when held proud and erect, reached Cam's shoulder. This morning Tad had dressed in his clean white shirt, buttoning it all the way up to the collar, and in the new woolen trousers they'd bought in Pascagoula last week. But he'd be outgrowing them soon, too. Campbell cast his eyes to the ground and concentrated on the familiar words.

"...For thine is the kingdom, the power, and the glory, for ever and ever. Amen."

The surrounding crowd of parishioners quietly repeated, "Amen."

After a respectful pause, the group began to disperse, many coming to shake Campbell's hand or pat him gently on the cheek, murmuring kind words of sorrow, commiseration and reassurance. He'd known most of these people all his life, and had tended their injuries and delivered their babies for the short time he practiced medicine here before the war. They were truly what St. Matthew must have envisioned as the salt of the earth.

"You will be staying around, now, won't you, Campbell?" Mrs. McPherson asked. "It would sure be nice to have a doctor close by again."

"You know the church could really use a good preacher again, son. It'd be real nice if you'd take over your Pa's pulpit." Mr. Connolly grinned at him around a wad of chewing tobacco, bringing to mind bittersweet memories of Jim Manning.

As the last of the congregation filtered away, Deacon and Mrs. Partee came up, and the man squeezed Cam's hand in both of his. "It certainly is good to have you back among us, Campbell."

Cam squeezed the man's hand in return. Partee had been one of his father's closest friends, and even in his own grief, had taken over leading the congregation after Emmett's death.

"I don't believe you've had a chance to meet my son, sir." Cam placed his hands on Tad's shoulders and introduced, "Tademus Co McCool."

With a wide smile, Tad stuck out his hand. "Pleasure to meet ya, Massah Partee, Miz Partee."

Partee took a small step back and his wife coughed delicately into her handkerchief. "Yes... boy... of course... "

Mrs. Partee interrupted the awkward silence. "We've set up a delicious pot luck down to the church, Campbell. Lucy baked three of those apple pies you used to like so much. You will be joining us, won't you?"

Campbell almost literally bit his tongue, but simply tipped his head and frowned at her.

"Well, you and the boy, of course," she quickly amended.

This was going to be a long road, Campbell realized. Hearts and minds didn't change overnight. He smiled obligingly at the woman. "We'd be delighted, Mrs. Partee. I could never pass up a piece of your daughter's pie or your fried chicken. Y'all go on ahead. We'd just like to spend a few more minutes here."

The Partees clucked their approval and headed off toward their wagon.

Tad shoved his hands into his pockets and kicked at the dirt. "They don't like me very much, do they, Camel?"

"They don't know you, Tad. Give them time."

"Just how much time you think they gonna need?"

"Patience, m'lad. We're entering a whole new world now."

Cam turned back to the fresh graves, now blanketed with roses, daisies, and goldenrod, all brought by the members of his father's congregation, the people who had called this little corner of Mississippi home for generations. The community that now wanted him to return and heal all their ills, both physical and spiritual.

He raised his eyes to gaze down the long lane that disappeared into the shadowy tunnel of live oaks that lined

Hanging Moss Road. When he'd walked away from that beach on Mobile Bay so many months ago, he'd been impelled by another purpose and another vision, and in the throes of his grief last night, that determination had taken hold of him again.

Tad knelt beside Davis' grave and picked up a daisy that had fallen from its companions. "Miz McCool and little Davis... they be home now, huh Camel?"

"Eventually, we all get there, Tad... as long as we believe."

After replacing the errant daisy, Tad gently rearranged a few of the roses into a neat bouquet. "You wasn't really born in a cemetery, was ya?"

A chuckled bubbled up in Cam's breast at Tad's reference to their earlier conversation. "No. Not a cemetery. A seminary."

"Well, it seems to me that you's born again, right here in this *cemetery*."

Campbell marveled at the wisdom coming from the mouth of a ten year old child. "Yeah, Tademus m'lad. I think you might be onto something." He stooped down beside Tad and gathered up a handful of the bright red, yellow and white flowers. "C'mon, son, let's go put these in some water, so maybe they'll last for a while. I have something I want to read to you."

He took Tad's hand and pulled him to his feet, and with the thorns of the roses poking into his other hand, he led Tad back to their tent. Pushed against the far end, between their two bedrolls, was the old chest that had been buried near the fireplace in the house that had burned. Opening the lid carefully on its cracking leather hinges, Cam lifted out the gilded portfolio that held his poetry. The verse he wanted was on top.

Tad sank to his bedroll, his mouth scrunched up in curiosity. Cam sat crosslegged opposite him and began to read.

MY SON

Of all the joys that one's life can bring,
There's none can surpass just one glorious thing:
It's the joining of two, in love and as one,
Which blesses them with a loving daughter or son.

So wondrous a miracle commended to us
Must surely be seen as God's ultimate trust -
A faith that in spite of man's feet of clay
Knows there's seed deep within that can purge him one day.

With all the weaknesses and frailties, the properties of flesh,
The spirit and soul with Him are immeshed.
As for it is written - through Christ I'm with you
He dwells among us this earthly life through -

'Til in its grand cycle we worthily complete;
And, rewarded in Heaven, we sit at His feet.
We reach to the stars, our quest never known,
But merely a glimpse of Him on His throne
Reassures that the life He's brought us to sow
Through our heirs, in Him, may continue to grow.

In His own true image, the Scriptures assure -
That's promise and more for man to endure
The trials and errors of so brief a stay,
As we comfort in the hope that we live life His way.

So as we prepare for our blessed event,
We recount all our fortunes through this life thus spent -
And praise Thee, dear God, and offer our prayers, too,
That those whom we beget may share Eternity with You.

Campbell thought all his tears had been shed, but now found a few more yet moistening his eyes. This time, though, they felt like tears of Joy... of Renewal... of Hope.

Cam knew this to be true. He knew Love had never left them. He recognized this to be...

but a new beginning...

MY MISSISSIPPI WILDFLOWER

THE BEAUTY OF YOUR SOUL
WILL CARRY YOU ONWARD
IN LOVE AND LIGHT
THE SWEETNESS OF YOUR SPIRIT
WILL CARRY YOU UPWARD
FOREVER AND BEYOND
THE MEMORY OF YOUR BEING
LIKE THE WILDFLOWERS OF SPRING
BLOOMS RENEWED IN OUR HEARTS

For
Shirley Faye

I love you, my dear, and I've loved you before,
but somehow within me I know -
That tomorrow and tomorrow and tomorrow and tomorrow -
I'll grow yet to love you still more

BB

A

CODA

LIFELINES

photography by BB

(Author's note: This poem was written in commemoration of the 9th Boone Family Reunion - a tradition established by 'my dear old Pa', the Very Reverend Doctor Boone, whose 'color' chosen was white. The reference in the poem to Ithamer Van Ransler's having been given many names then called none comes for his having throughout his life been addressed by his initials, I.V.)

GENERATIONS

When we were children and all was new
  We had much to draw upon -
For in our house love did abound,
  To send us far beyond -
To seek our destinies through life,
  No matter where they led -
And shield our way against all strife -
  As all our dreams were fed.

United in Holy Bonds of Love,
  Mama and Papa did so beget -
Their first-born, a male,
  Whom they dubbed Fred,
And he did oh surely fret.

Then came Albert to make it four
  As our family began to grow.
The Lord saw fit to give Papa help
  For all the fields to sow.

GENERATIONS

Next born was Roy and what a boy!
      He grew to tower tall -
And built a family to carry on
      Far beyond his earthly life's stall.

A little girl, Myrle, next blessed our home,
      Though briefly she did stay -
'Twas only a few years she lingered there,
      And then was on her way.

Then along came Gilbert of whom they'd say,
      'He most resembles Ed' -
Yet clearly seen among all offspring,
      The Boone stamp was left in red.

The next to grace, or is that the right word,
      While his color chosen was white -
Norman Udell did come to fill our well
      Of Faith to keep us right.

Following him you see was Ruby Lee,
      Welcomed among so many boys -
Papa's field hands had already numbered five -
      Now Mama had an ally for domestic joys.

A third daughter, Lois, passed through our house,
      Like Myrle for just a while,
But she made her presence a sweetening touch
      Before traveling that final mile.

(continued on next page)

GENERATIONS

(continued from previous page)

Then Ithamer Van Ransler was the unlikely tag
　　　Attached the sixth Boone son.
Mama and Papa decided to give him many names,
　　　Then promptly called him none.

So next came Bonnie, our bouncy lass,
　　　Given the first Boone double alliteration -
And lifted the scales females to males:
　　　Two daughters now and six Boone sons.

Then one last time Mama became with child,
　　　Curtis would be the seventh son,
And legend has Papa echoing his words,
　　　"No more here that doctor will run!"

So these beginnings we have in common to share
　　　As on this ninth anniversary we gather,
Praising Thee, dear God, our Heavenly Father,
　　　For things which really matter.

MY SON, THE TEENAGER

The stages of life, unfolding as we grow -
Lead through an adventure of which little we know.

And now, my fine son, you've matured to a teen
With your life more a blessing than I might've hoped or foreseen.

Your richness of spirit, mature beyond your years -
You're a friend to your elders as well as to your peers.

And I as your father would have you to know -
My devotion for you reaches beyond what might show.

There are absolutes, assurances, certainties and such,
But they wane in comparison to my love felt so much.

The continuity of generations, the passage they say -
Enables a man to live another day.

Well, I would contend the mantle you wear
Is girded by honor, gentle thoughtfulness, and care.

We've experienced a lot as father and son -
Weathered any and all storms then basked in the sun.

Now as you encounter your years as a teen -
Anticipation builds upon each and every dream.

And as you move on to adventures untold,
May you do so in faith God's plan will unfold.

MY NEPHEW

Seems not long ago your dad
*   got off a plane in L.A.*
And flashed a picture of his newborn son -
*   there was little more to say.*

At first opportunity I hastened back
*   for an 'in person' visit with you*
And, holding you gently, whispered in your ear -
*   "I love you, my little nephew."*

The next thing I knew you were sitting up
*   or so your Mother claimed you to be -*
Though to me you looked more like a tripod
*   with your head on the floor between your knees.*

Then time would appear to lap dissolve
*   to find you pedaling your green machine*
As if H.G. Wells had commissioned you
*   to propel us through time, it seemed.*

We would, however, have a moment here and there
*   for hurling a football pass or two -*
Before your vehicle had become a regular bike
*   and your setting "Norman Rockwell" true.*

Seems apt to pause right here to praise
*   your Mother and Dad for all their giving -*
And count among God's many blessings to you
*   home and hearth and family and living.*

Thusly, on that note of offering thanks
*   I'd certainly extend mine to you -*
For all the dimensions you've brought my life
*   since first christening me 'Uncle Bredo'.*

Next we discover along with athletic prowess
*   there's a scholar as well who is surging -*
So we're called upon to computerize our brain
*   as riddles from your mouth start emerging.*

Now, as you enter a new era of youth,
*   The indomitable phase known as 'teens' -*
I trust God will guide you the rest of the way,
*   granting you fullness of life and all that it means.*

MY SISTER

On this day as I recall so well,
'Twas back in '47 -
I had an experience never known before -
Taking me as close as I'd ever been to Heaven.

The Chancellor and I strolled home from school,
When he turned and commented to me,
"By now you've a baby brother or sis,"
And in tyme I'd come see,

That little girl
Who'd indeed complete
Our loving pham-a-lee.
"We'll name her Rebecca," I volunteered,
Phrom a movie that I knew.
But then this is not just about me, my dear,
But rather all about you!

Happy Birthday, Big Sis!!!
Your Wannabee Brother

RETIREMENT

Some say the word is retirement,
That time after active years;
Yet, Autumn would seem best to describe
This season laced with laughter and tears.

It's a time when all around us
Reflects the fruit of more productive years -
A special season to savor life's nectars
Made sweeter by fulfilled careers.

For like nature, life has its seasons -
With Autumn's retirement being our reward,
After oft blistering toils of Summer
And before the ultimate rest brings accord.

Still how can we think of not living
With the promise of Winter so near -
When that final season of wintery white
Sheds the darkness of death and all fear?

While the cycle of life as we've known it
Will have completed its earthly confines,
It will have earned us passage from these seasons four
Into a Springtime with our God Devine.

So considering life's beginning as springtime,
Followed by its challenges of Summer to face -
Let's retire in our Autumn to ponder
Our Savior Who's prepared us our place.

This Winter promise of new life will spring forth,
Radiating its glorious hue -
We'll be home with our Heavenly Father,
Who'll redeem us with life with Him anew.

STREAMS OF CONSCIOUSNESS

IMPRESSIONS

Our time together has grown so brief -
One begins to wonder where lies the relief.

But when the heart holds years' fond dreams -
The warmth of love flows ever still in streams.

Yet lest we may forget the passion -
Let n'er these memories become a ration.

For love's bittersweet pain may pass -
Only when no seed was left to last.

WHITE MOMENTS

There are only so many 'firsts' in life -
Those rare and beautiful 'White Moments' -
There're certainly too few to leave to chance -
By treating them merely as components.

Let's then guard and cherish each brand new experience -
With awareness that it is most grand -
Instead of quickly passing the moment by -
With blasé thoughts of its coming again.

UNRAVELLINGS

Love, truth, beauty -
These are <u>MY</u> gems -
Allegiance, too.

Hate, dishonesty, frowns -
These are someone's whims. -
Don't ask me. . . whose.

ABJECT OBJECTIVE

Through generations what legacy
Will mankind choose to leave?
A body wasted - a soul that's lost?
Well, those must surely grieve.

Let's span the time that's ours to live
And show life's innate goodness -
Instead of foul and selfish ways
Which net us 'dirty business.'

LIFE'S SWEET DREAMS

When lonely depths
Of night we reach -
There're endless tides
Which find no beach.

The wind is warm
Or so it seems -
Unless it's felt
Only in our dreams.

SELF

Identity can be no crisis -
Only when there is none.

THE HUMAN TANDEM

In despair...

      to hope.

             In elation...

                  to sober.

In traversity...

      to excel.

             In discovery...

                  to quest.

In anxiety...

      to triumph.

             In completion...

                  to hunger.

In diversity...

      to understand.

             In allegiance...

                  to qualify.

In bonds...

      to free.

             In knowledge...

                  to thirst.

In defeat...

      to emerge.

             In faith...

                  to reaffirm.

In doubt...

      to reassure.

             In glory...

                  to deserve.

THE HUMAN TANDEM

In wrong...

     to right.

          In time...

               to endure.

In self...

     to recognize

          In love...

               to give

In grief...

     to mend.

          In salvation...

               to earn.

             In Him to believe.

Be these the ambitions of mankind -
For surely they must be the expectations of Him...

             From God.

Help me, I pray - to know the way.

             Amen.

A THANK YOU TO MY CHARTER FOUR FANS

T'was the night before Christmas
In the year '91,
And I sat by the tree,
Just me with my son.

The lights were aglow,
Shining ever so bright.
The frost out was forming,
Giving reflections in the night.

A setting rich indeed
With the season's message of love -
And thoughts no longer earthbound,
Being lifted to Heights above.

When what to our listening ears
Did we perchance to hear -
But the faint, puttering sound
Of a UPS truck drawing near.

The driver then leapt
From his seat to the ground,
Wearing colors not white
But autumn haze brown.

He raced to our door,
A package in hand -
And smiled as he recognized
"Hey - you are the man!"

A THANK YOU TO MY CHARTER FOUR FANS

The "B's" accepted the box,
Giving a Holiday Greet.
The driver turned on his heels
With a "It's a pleasure to meet."

We returned to our tree,
Placing under it there
This piece of the past
From those who must care.

The next morn we would save
'Til after the rest -
This gift that we'd open.
It'd have to be best.

So just that we did do,
And opened it last -
To bring to the present
This piece of the past.

While time is a reference
This life must respect,
Film freezes some moments
We'd like to protect.

So from these treasured episodes
Of GARRISON'S GORILLAS -
"Chief" with his son
Would shed any peccadilloes

(continued on next page)

A THANK YOU TO MY CHARTER FOUR FANS

(continued from previous page)

And offer heartfelt, deep thanks
To Linda, Lil, Carol and Rae -
For their generous, kind thoughtfulness
In preserving for us this day.

Of Christmas '91
The record will show -
Special friends extended love
In ways few may ever know.

So the "B's" thank you, dear ones,
So faithful and true -
For twenty-six movies
But for most of all - YOU.

CALENDAR VERSES

January's promise, a slate that's clean—
we forge ahead toward experiences unseen.

February warms those hearts in love—
with heavenly promises from our Lord above.

March brings a wind to encourage us toward
good times ahead which will bring reward.

April can offer fresh, gentle rains so
that on the horizon we see a rainbow.

May launches in spring with life that is new—
there's a message right here for me and for you.

June brings us warmth from the sun so near,
and one comforts in knowing there's nothing to fear.

July ushers in year's second half,
and for some a son—from a bull a calf?!

August bridges the seasons—times then and those now,
we continue the journey without asking how.

September sweeps over, and leaves are then shed.
In glorious hues, our visions are fed.

October can chill right down to the bone—
our senses so keen, but we're never alone.

November is due, and winter sets in
with a dusting of white as though purging of all sin.

December arrives, and the faithful can know
that love and hope will forever grow.

LYRICS TO THE THEME

In times so hard and troublesome to define,
rode two unlikely to have their lives entwine.
Their purpose was such though they didn't have much,
their way oh surely they'd find.

They vowed one the other they'd be each other's brother;
yet this lesson to learn would melt in the sun -
if Hope's wings should die from their flutter.
Their path was not straight though void of all hate -
while bringing them to see promised all Eternity,
they mustn't challenge this fate.

Once in a while they may stumble but 'fore friendship could crumble -
they'd rally around on far firmer ground -
and in sharing life's glories they'd humble.

They rode on together like birds of a feather -
toward meeting a common cause,
demonstrating how man while serving his span -
must do so in respect for God's laws.

(continued on next page)

LYRICS TO THE THEME

(continued from previous page)

For only then can he find being of truly sound mind -
he's earned right to life's everlasting pause.

"Preacher and Co" was their branded logo,
and proudly they carried it high -
to prove to the world varied flags may unfurl -
still kinship must grow by and by.

<u>STEPHEN BOYD TO BRENDON BOONE IN LIFE:</u>

"I hope you'll not much longer be wasted."

<u>CAMPBELL TO TAD IN PREACHER AND CO:</u>

"It's not for us to know, one way or another, just
what God might intend for our lives. We just must
hope that His will be done."

now through a glass darkly

while the best is yet to come

Lovingly edited and illustrated by
our most creative
Beehive Enterprises
in-house graphic arts designer,
Margretta
(Maggie, My Musette Mag-Jag)
Parker-Hearn

BEE TYMELY

Our only measure in this dimension called life -
We refer to as tyme and it's filled with strife.

Still we're offered a Way to another day -
Of wakening from this death with its feet of clay.

Awaits us is a Glory our minds can't conceive -
With our mission while here in Him to believe.

And share with as many other souls as we might -
A Beacon of Hope from God's Beam of Light.